Praise for James Morrow

"The most provocative satiric voice in science fiction."
— *Washington Post*

"Widely regarded as the foremost satirist associated with the SF and Fantasy field."
— *SF Site*

"Morrow understands theology like a theologian and psychology like a psychologist, but he writes like an angel."
— Richard Elliott Friedman, author of
The Hidden Book in the Bible

On the Theodore Sturgeon Memorial Award-winning novella *Shambling Towards Hiroshima*

"Sharp-edged, delightfully batty...skillfully mingling real and imaginary characters with genuinely hilarious moments."
— *Kirkus*

"Morrow liberally salts the yarn with real Hollywood horror-movie personnel, Jewish showbiz snark, and gut-wrenching regret for the bomb. As usual for Morrow, a stellar performance."
— *Booklist*

"[A] tour-de-force of razor-sharp wit...packs a big wallop..."
— *SciFi Dimensions*

"Morrow is the only author who comes close to Vonnegut's caliber. Like Vonnegut, Morrow shrouds his work in science fiction, but the real story is always man's infinite capacities for love and for evil."

—*The Stranger*

"Witty, playful...reminiscent of *Watchmen*..."

—*Strange Horizons*

"In the tradition of *Dr. Strangelove*...even as you're laughing you're not sure you should be."

—Amazon.com *Omnivoracious*

"James Morrow's bizarrely funny new book *Shambling Towards Hiroshima* turns the usual Godzilla paradigm on its head: Instead of being inspired by the horrors of nuclear war, Godzilla is its herald."

—*io9.com*

"This is what we have come to expect from Morrow: intelligent, thoughtful, dark comedy with real bite—and in this case radioactive breath."

—*The New York Review of Science Fiction*

On *The Philosopher's Apprentice*

"[A] tumultuous take on humanity, philosophy and ethics that is as hilarious as it is outlandish."

—*Kirkus*

"Morrow's world is one where ideas matter so much they come lurching to life as intellectual Frankenstein creatures. In *The Philosopher's Apprentice* they are wickedly hilarious—and they can break our hearts and scare us silly."

—*Denver Post*

"Morrow is even more inventive than Vonnegut and has Vonnegut's willingness to milk every sacred cow in the pasture... but *The Philosopher's Apprentice* is not just a collection of comic gestures. It can be unexpectedly moving, with scenes of great literary ambiguity."

—*Cleveland Plain Dealer*

On *The Last Witchfinder*

"James Morrow's novel about early American witchcraft pulls off so many dazzling feats of literary magic that in a different century he'd have been burned at the stake."

—*Washington Post*

"This impeccably researched, highly ambitious novel—nine years in the writing—is a triumph of historical fiction."

—*Booklist*

"Grim and gorgeous, earthy and erudite as well, Morrow's *Witchfinder* woos readers with a secularist vision of reason triumphant, rewarding its following richly, giving them all the world and ample time in which to enjoy it."

—*Seattle Times*

On *The Cat's Pajamas*

"His latest collection demonstrates that his rapier wit has lost none of its edge as it encompasses twisted scenarios ranging from Martians invading Central Park to having the fates of other worlds rest upon the scores of American football games.... All the stories manifest Morrow's penchant for exploring the dark underbelly of technological promise and extracting quirky moral conundrums. Morrow's fans will revel, and first-time readers may find his grim humor making fans of them, too."

—*Booklist*

"Far more entertaining than most of that tedious stuff you've been forcing yourself to read."

—*Fantastic Reviews*

"Amply displays [Morrow's] ability to juggle absurdity, tragedy, irony and outrage..."

—*Locus*

Also by James Morrow

Novels
The Wine of Violence (1981)
The Continent of Lies (1984)
This Is the Way the World Ends (1985)
Only Begotten Daughter (1990)
City of Truth (1990)
The Last Witchfinder (2006)
The Philosopher's Apprentice (2008)
Shambling Towards Hiroshima (2009)
Galápagos Regained (forthcoming 2015)

The Godhead Trilogy
Towing Jehovah (1994)
Blameless in Abaddon (1996)
The Eternal Footman (1999)

Short Story Collections
Bible Stories for Adults (1996)
The Cat's Pajamas (2004)

The Madonna and the Starship
Copyright © 2014 by James Morrow

Cover art copyright © 2014 by Elizabeth Story
Cover and interior design by Elizabeth Story

Tachyon Publications
1459 18th Street #139
San Francisco, CA 94107
(415) 285-5615
tachyon@tachyonpublications.com

www.tachyonpublications.com
smart science fiction & fantasy

Series Editor: Jacob Weisman
Project Editor: Jill Roberts

ISBN 13: 978-1-61696-159-6

Printed in the United States of America by Worzalla

First Edition: 2014
9 8 7 6 5 4 3 2 1

The Madonna and the Starship

THE MADONNA AND THE STARSHIP

JAMES MORROW

TACHYON | SAN FRANCISCO

To my nephews,
Ian Loefgren and Wit Kaczanowski,
this latest effort from
Uncle Wonder

1.

UNCLE WONDER BUILDS A JET ENGINE

X minus ten seconds and counting! Nine, eight, seven! Step lively, cosmic cadets! Six, five, four! Time to scramble aboard the space schooner TRITON! Good job, cadets, you made it! Three, two, one ... BLAST OFF with BROCK BARTON AND HIS ROCKET RANGERS! Brought to you by Kellogg's Sugar Corn Pops, with the sweetenin' already on it, and by Ovaltine, the hot chocolaty breakfast drink schoolteachers recommend! And now, stalwart star sailors, let's race on up to the bridge, where Brock and his crew are about to receive an assignment that will hurtle them pell-mell into the dreaded "Coils of Terror," chapter one of this week's exciting adventure, THE COBRA KING OF GANYMEDE!

If I were a nine-year-old kid becalmed in the cultural doldrums of postwar America, nothing would have thrilled me more than the voice of Jerry Korngold announcing an impending episode of *Brock Barton and His Rocket Rangers.* Every Monday, Wednesday, and Friday afternoon, at four o'clock precisely, this indefatigable off-screen TV host delivered the program's opening signature, exhorting young viewers to enter a sacred and forbidden zone. Follow me to the throbbing heart of the cosmos, boys and girls. Come hither to infinity.

As fate would have it, however, in the early fifties I could not accept Jerry's entrancing invitation, partly because I was no longer a child but mostly because I happened to be the head writer of *Brock Barton and His Rocket Rangers.* I liked my job. Just as our show enabled kids to fantasize that they were star sailors, so did my scripting duties allow me to imagine I was a playwright, though I knew perfectly well that nobody was about to confuse a space schooner called the *Triton* with a streetcar named *Desire.*

While my primary *Brock Barton* obligation was to crank out a triad of weekly episodes, including a cliff-hanging climax for chapters one and two, I was further charged with writing and starring in a ten-minute epilogue to each installment, the popular *Uncle Wonder's Attic* segment. Cut to me, Kurt Jastrow, a.k.a. Uncle Wonder, an endearing old tinkerer in a cardigan sweater. (I played the role behind an artificial grizzled beard and equally fake eyebrows.) Nestled in his attic workshop, Uncle Wonder has just finished watching the latest

Brock Barton chapter with a neighborhood kid, freckle-faced Andy Tuckerman. The absentminded eccentric flips off his bulky Motorola TV and chats with Andy about the episode, and before long the boy pipes up with an astute question concerning some scientific aspect of the *Brock Barton* universe. (I tried to leaven the show's bedrock implausibility with flashes of real physics and chemistry.) After rummaging around in the attic, Uncle Wonder finds the necessary materials, then proceeds to address the boy's perplexity through a science experiment.

Under normal circumstances, the Monday, November 9, 1953, *Brock Barton* chapter called "Coils of Terror" would not have lodged in my memory. It was neither better nor worse than my usual attempt to write a script poised on the proper side of the rift that separates exhilarating junk from irredeemable dreck. As it happened, though, "Coils of Terror" occasioned my first interaction with the Qualimosans—I speak now of by-God extraterrestrials, complete with crustacean physiognomy, insectile eyes, and an antisocial agenda—and so I can easily discuss that episode without benefit of a kinescope or other tangible record of the broadcast. Don't touch that dial.

Historians today call it the Golden Age of television, but for those of us who were actually there, it was nothing of the kind. Cardboard sets, primitive special effects, subsistence budgets: we were living in the Stone Age of the medium, and we knew it. True, my employer, NBC, did a classy job of informing viewers about current events—radio had taught them the art of gathering and broadcasting the news—and the network took a justifiable pride in its anthologies of dramas written expressly for the cathode-ray tube, but when it came to *Brock Barton* and other kiddie fare, the National Broadcasting Company was primarily concerned with holding down costs and sucking up advertising revenues.

That said, I was not complaining, at least not to anyone who exercised power at the network. Although the thought of spending my life writing juvenile space operas depressed me, I knew I had a good thing going, especially when I considered how far I'd come: all the way from Mom and Dad's central Pennsylvania dairy farm to New York's most celebrated bohemian enclave, Greenwich Village—an odyssey whose primary detour had found me in Allied-occupied Japan, working with my fellow U.S. Army conscripts to remind the deeply spiritual citizens of shrine-laden Kyoto that reconvening the Second World War would be a bad idea. When people asked me why I'd decided to seek my fortune in New York, I always replied, "I came for the trees," an unconvincing answer—there are many more trees in central Pennsylvania than in the five boroughs—to which I immediately appended a clarification. "That is, I came for the greatest of all the good things trees give us, better than fruit or shade, better than birds. I speak of pulp."

Such a savory word. Without pulp there was no *Amazing Stories*. Without pulp, no *Weird Tales*, no *Planet Stories*, *Thrilling Wonder Stories*, *Galaxy*, or *Astounding Science Fiction*. Most especially there was no *Andromeda*, la crème du fantastique, a monthly compendium of *Gedanken* experiments clothed in the regalia of science fiction. During my adolescence I must have read over three hundred *Andromeda* stories, an educational experience for which I can thank my father's bachelor brother.

Uncle Wyatt made his living teaching English at Central High in Philadelphia, and whenever Mom, Dad, and I visited his Germantown row house, I was allowed to descend into the basement and pore through his literary treasures, which included not only pulp fiction but also *Captain Billy's Whiz Bang*, *The Police Gazette*, and the occasional girlie slick, featuring what we now call soft-core pornography. My uncle's grotto smelled of coal dust, kerosene, and fungus, a fragrance that, owing to its association with his moldering periodicals, was the most exquisite I'd ever known. While the magazines devoted to ruthless pirates, fearless explorers, and daredevil pilots engaged my interest, it was the science-fiction pulps that truly mesmerized me, to the point where I decided that writing stories and novelettes for *Andromeda* must be the best possible way to earn a living. (This was before I understood that no human being had ever supported himself in this fashion.) At first my commitment to an extraterrestrial vocation was equivocal, but then one afternoon Uncle Wyatt joined me in his cave of wonders, set his palm on an *Andromeda* stack, and said, "The church of cosmic astonishment, Kurt. It's the only religion you'll ever need."

"Church?" I said, fixing on the topmost cover, an exquisite image of a rocketship approaching a double-ringed planet, one loop paralleling the equator, the second passing through the north and south poles: dubious physics, but transcendent iconography. "Religion?"

"Indeed," said my father's brother, laying an affirming hand on my shoulder. Eventually, of course, I would transmogrify my memories of Wyatt Jastrow into a character called Uncle Wonder. "I only wish its scripture were better written."

My course was now set, and in time my allegiance to the church of cosmic astonishment found me boarding the fabulous streamlined Crusader in Reading Terminal, detraining in Jersey City, and taking the ferry across the bay to New York Harbor—for how better to pursue my intended career than to pitch my tent within hailing distance of Saul Silver, renowned editor of *Andromeda*? I spent the next five weeks at the Gotham Grand, a fleabag hotel on the Lower East Side, surviving at first on $100 in cash from Uncle Wyatt, then scraping by on the wages and tips I received from waiting tables in Stuyvesant Town. Among my fellow Gotham Grand tenants were two other apprentice bohemians—Eliot Thornhill, a budding actor from Delaware, and Lenny Margolis, an aspiring "cultural journalist" from New Jersey—and one day the three of us decided that, if we pooled our resources, we could rent an apartment in Greenwich Village.

When I agreed to cast my lot with the thespian and the trend spotter, I didn't realize the package would include the complete *Encyclopaedia Britannica* Lenny got for winning a national high-school essay contest. No sooner had we moved into 378 Bleecker Street, apartment 4R, than Lenny arranged for his parents to deliver all twenty-four volumes to our doorstep, a fount of knowledge from which he allowed me to drink promiscuously, especially after I taught him how to buy condoms at the corner barber shop. (Unlike most consumers of Uncle Wyatt's girlie slicks, I read the advice columns.) Throughout my years of roughing it in the Village, Lenny's *Encyclopaedia Britannica* became the college education Mom and Dad could never afford to give me.

Against all odds, Saul Silver bought the first story I submitted to *Andromeda*, "Brainpan Alley," spun from the *Britannica*'s account of Sigmund Freud's theories. A mad scientist, seeking to liberate his mind from the

7

fetters of both moral convention and animal instinct, transplants his superego into a bronze statue of the fourth-century heretical monk Pelagius, even as he relocates his id to a stuffed orangutan in the American Museum of Natural History. As fate and plot contrivance would have it, the statue comes to life, likewise the taxidermal ape, and the two creatures spend the rest of the story alternately drubbing each other and making life miserable for the hapless genius who evicted them from his psyche.

"Dear Mr. Jastrow, you are an intellectual snob," Saul Silver's letter to me began. "However, the scene of the monk sucker-punching the orangutan was too delicious to pass up. Enclosed please find a check for $120. Sincerely, S. Silver. P.S. Send me more."

That night I took my roommates out for sirloin steaks and beer at Chumley's on Christopher Street. Eliot vowed to reciprocate the instant he got a part in a Broadway show, as did Lenny if and when an editor took a chance on his journalistic talents. Before the year was out, both promises were kept, for April found Eliot playing a palace guard in *The King and I*, and in June the *Brooklynite* paid Lenny $250 to write "The Celluloid Insurgents," a feature about the phenomenon of "underground movies." (He also got to keep the ancient Bell & Howell Filmosound projector with which he'd studied the 16mm curiosities in question.) But neither the Rodgers & Hammerstein roast beef nor the guerilla-cinema brisket had tasted half so succulent as the protein that accrued to my *Andromeda* triumph.

Two more sales followed apace. "Knight Takes Bishop" told of Ivan Gerasimenko, chess master of the galaxy, who relinquishes his title when bested by an alien-built computer. On his deathbed Ivan learns that the uncanny machine's program consists exclusively of his own preferred strategies and tactics, and so he passes away a happy man, realizing that he didn't lose the final tournament, for the winner was his cybernetic self. (Everyone was reading Norbert Wiener that year.) "The Pleistocene Spies" was my first attempt at political satire, the target being the persecution of Julius and Ethel Rosenberg, currently on trial for espionage, as they'd allegedly given away the secret of the atomic bomb to the Soviets. A primitive future society built on the ashes of a global nuclear war becomes locked in an arms race with an adjacent community. Two canny savages named Jurgus and Elthea are persecuted by the United River Tribes for supposedly passing the flint-spearhead formula to the Collectivized Mud Tribes. I thought my story quite clever, and so did Saul, but then the Rosenbergs went to the electric chair, an event that made orphans of their two sons, and suddenly "The Pleistocene Spies" didn't seem remotely amusing.

I sold one more story to Saul that year, an androids-in-revolt allegory called "Rusted Justice," and then the rejection letters started arriving, not only from

Andromeda but also *Astounding, Galaxy, Weird Tales*, and even *Planet Stories*. It was obvious that the three-way intersection of Uncle Wyatt's basement, my fevered cerebrum, and the *Encyclopaedia Britannica* would not reliably cover my share of the Bleecker Street rent. So I penned a science-fiction teleplay for children, outlined four follow-up episodes, and started pounding the midtown-Manhattan pavements, hoping that my *Andromeda* track record might land me an interview with some TV potentates.

I couldn't get past the receptionist at the Dumont Network, and CBS proved equally impervious, but somehow I wrangled a thirty-minute audience at NBC with Walter Spalding, head of programming, and George Cates, the marketing director, who listened attentively as I described a series that would give ABC's *Planet Patrol* a run for its money. (The executives were especially intrigued by my idea of concluding each episode with a geezer doing science experiments in his attic.) I left the meeting with a feather in my cap—not merely a feather, a billowing plume, and a credit to go with it: Kurt Jastrow, assistant writer and associate development chief for *Brock Barton and His Rocket Rangers*. Mr. Spalding would function as executive producer. Mr. Cates would corral a couple of sponsors. The universe was my oyster.

I was not long on the job before realizing that NBC's new outer-space series had neither a head writer nor a development chief. When it came to penning the scripts and defining the program's underlying sociological and political assumptions, *Brock Barton* would be a one-man band, Kurt Jastrow receiving $210 a week to play all the brass, woodwinds, and percussion, though my resourceful director, Floyd Cox, and my ingenious special-effects technician, Mike Zipser, could also claim credit for the show's success. While the contract required me to run every teleplay past my bosses, they never suggested deletions or changes, as Mr. Spalding rarely bothered to read anything I wrote—the steady stream of fan letters convinced him to leave my bailiwick alone—and Mr. Cates read only far enough to verify that the hero would appear on camera for the umpteenth time eating a bowl of Sugar Corn Pops and, later, downing a glass of Ovaltine.

I quickly learned that the fraternity of television writers was divided into two camps. For the self-proclaimed "linguals," live TV was the bastard child of that venerable art form called radio drama. According to this school, dialogue and narration were the *sine qua non* of the new medium, and it was always better to paint a scene with words, thereby engaging the viewer's imagination, than to attempt an on-screen flying dragon, spouting volcano, or sinking ship, because whatever the technicians devised was bound to look ridiculous.

The rival faction, the "ocularists," located the essence of television in the camera's lens, not the mind's eye. True, the medium did not allow for Hollywood-style opticals or stop-motion animation, but you could still employ models, miniatures, and painted backdrops. Indeed, the low-fidelity picture tube often made such images appear vaguely authentic. And, of course, thanks to the switching device in the control room, the director could take the various cathode-ray streams arriving from the studio floor, their contents having been dictated to the cameramen via headsets, and blend them into exotic composites. Through the switcher's magic, an ordinary lizard could become a dinosaur—a simple matter of mixing camera one's shot of a live iguana with camera two's shot of a prospector cowering on a desert set—just as a sun-struck vampire could be turned into a skeleton, or a couple of actors in diving gear transported to the gates of an underwater city.

Ultimately I pledged my allegiance to the linguals. I was a published author, after all, a professional whose fiction had occasioned seven fan letters in *Andromeda*. And yet in writing my weekly quota of TV episodes, I always tried to give the ocularists their due—Floyd Cox and Mike Zipser favored this approach—and the adventure called "The Cobra King of Ganymede" was no exception.

The plot had the villainous ruler in question, the

notorious Argon Drakka, threatening our solar system by breeding space-dwelling pythons of ever-increasing size, eventually creating a serpent who could gird a planet, Midgard-like, so that the inhabitants faced an unhappy choice between doing Drakka's bidding and having their world crushed like a tennis ball in a vise. Monday's chapter, "Coils of Terror," found Galaxy Central ordering the space schooner to the moon of Jupiter called Ganymede, so Brock could investigate the rumor that Drakka was experimenting with extraterrestrial reptiles. Before embarking on the assignment, Brock collected his crew on the bridge of the *Triton* (an elaborate set that filled an entire quadrant of Studio One), including his fearless first lieutenant, Lance Rawlings; his prepossessing second lieutenant, Wendy Evans, a.k.a. the love interest; a slap-happy ensign, Ducky Malloy; a humanoid robot, Cotter Pin; and a talking gorilla, Sylvester Simian, whose intellect had been augmented through accelerated evolution. Shortly after the *Triton* landed on Ganymede, Drakka unleashed one of his creatures-in-progress, a serpent of intermediate immensity that dutifully sinuated across the sands toward the space schooner and wrapped itself around the hull. (I felt confident Mike Zipser could coax a live garter snake into embracing our *Triton* model.) Cut to a commercial: a *non sequitur* shot of Brock, now mysteriously relocated to Galaxy Central, enjoying a bowl of Kellogg's Sugar Corn Pops. "And remember, kids, it's got the sweetenin' already on it!" Cut back to Ganymede. With a reverberant prerecorded hiss the snake constricted. The schooner buckled. Girders snapped. Rivets popped loose—and then, suddenly, the monster's head breached the viewport, threatening to sink a huge pointy tooth into Wendy: a composite shot fusing camera one's close-up of a snake-head puppet with camera two's image of the *Triton* bridge. Fade-out. Cut to Brock doing an Ovaltine commercial. Dissolve to title card, FANGS OF DEATH.

"Be sure to tune in Wednesday for 'Fangs of Death,'" exhorted Jerry Korngold, "chapter two of 'The Cobra King of Ganymede'!"

Up in the control room, Floyd ordered the usual dissolve to camera three: the familiar attic set, including a Motorola TV displaying, via a closed-circuit feed, the title card, FANGS OF DEATH. (The rabbit ears were just for show.) After Uncle Wonder—yours truly, Kurt Jastrow—deactivated the picture tube, a fresh title card, UNCLE WONDER'S ATTIC, appeared over a close-up of the tinkerer's acolyte, Andy Tuckerman.

Smiling benevolently, itching beneath my ersatz beard and eyebrows, I paced around amid the canonical collection of attic bric-a-brac—dressmaker's dummy, steamer trunk, hurricane lantern, grandfather clock—and addressed Andy in reassuring tones. "Wendy sure has gotten herself in a peck of trouble, hasn't she? But I'm not worried, Andy, are you?"

An exciting chapter, to be sure, though not free of the disasters to which live television was heir. Ducky Malloy had bobbled his first line, "Not Ganymede again, their bars serve the worst orange juice in the Milky Way," which came out, "Not Ganymede again, their oranges serve the worst Milky Way bars in the galaxy." (We'd be hearing from the Mars Candy Company about that one.) While coiling itself around the *Triton*, the snake had snapped off a stabilizer, betraying the space schooner as a mere balsa-wood prop. And when the reptile's head penetrated the bridge, Lance Rawlings had glanced at the floor monitor, seen the composite, and started laughing uncontrollably, forcing Sylvester to provide his lines from memory.

"Brock will save the day!" declared Andy. I was not alone in my lack of affection for this unctuous child. Everyone at the network thought he was a pill. "He always comes through in the nick of time!"

"Right you are! Say, Andy, have you ever wondered what makes the *Triton*'s shuttle go zooming across the sky?"

"I'm guessin' it uses a jet engine!"

"Yep!" Sidling toward my worktable, I pulled on a pair of canvas gloves. "And it happens we can build a jet engine right here"—I stared into camera three, its tally-light ablaze—"and so can all you kids at home."

"Gee willikers!" exclaimed Andy.

"We start with an empty cylindrical ice-cream tub."

By now the camera-two operator had wheeled his rig into Uncle Wonder's sector of the studio, so that, as I identified the engine's components, Floyd could reveal each in close-up. "We also need an aluminum pie-plate, a basin of room-temperature water, two short drinking-straw segments, a lump of putty, a pair of kitchen tongs, and some chunks of dry ice." Cut to camera three: a midshot of Uncle Wonder. I winked at the lens. "Kids, you can get your dry ice from the man who drives your Popsicle truck. Popsicle brings you *Wild West Roundup* every Tuesday and Thursday afternoons at four o'clock here on your local NBC station."

"I see you're wearin' gloves," said Andy.

"You bet I am. Never touch dry ice with your bare hands."

I equipped the kid with his own gloves, and then we got to work. Under my supervision Andy punched two holes on opposite sides of the ice-cream tub, then inserted the straw segments, securing them with putty and curling them in opposite directions. I filled our cardboard jet engine a quarter of the way with warm water, rested it on the pie-plate, and set the plate afloat in the basin.

"Go ahead, Andy, fuel the engine."

The kid seized the tongs and—*plop, plop, plop*—dropped three chunks of dry ice into the tub.

"Here's how our machine works," I said, fitting the lid back over the tub. "The heat of the engine-water causes the dry ice to dissolve quickly. The vapor escapes through the straw segments in two complementary streams of thrust. Our turbine reacts by—"

Right on cue, the floating tub-and-plate arrangement began rotating in the basin.

"Spinning!"

"Gollywhompers, that's swell!" said Andy. "I think I'll go home and make a jet engine of my own!" Whistling, he headed for the door. "Mind if I borrow these gloves? Safety first, right, Uncle Wonder?"

"Of course you can borrow 'em! Safety first!"

Dissolve to end title. Fade-out. Cut to NBC logo.

The operators of cameras two and three lost no time switching off their rigs and leaving the floor—they were scheduled to cover *Sing-Along Circus* in Studio Three— even as the audio engineer killed the boom mike and the lighting director doused the kliegs. Though free to go home, I elected to hang around the deserted attic set and practice Wednesday's science experiment.

Because the next chapter of "Cobra King" involved Brock detonating a bomb inside a dormant volcano, I'd decided to demonstrate why bakeries and flour mills sometimes exploded. The setup included a small funnel resting inside an empty paint can with a perforated bottom. A rubber tube snaked beneath the can, one end bare, the other suckling the funnel's spout. Before Andy's popping eyes, I would fill the funnel with flour, place a burning candle in the paint can, seal it with a metal lid, and exhale into the tube, forcing the white powder into a fateful rendezvous with the candle flame.

The rehearsal went rather too well. No sooner did I perform the requisite puff than a detonation rocked the attic set, wrenching off the paint-can lid and hurling it into the hurricane lantern—*smash, crash, tinkle, tinkle*— even as a fireball blossomed atop the worktable. My first thought: if my trial explosion had intruded on the live broadcast spilling from Studio Three, the *Sing-Along Circus* people would never speak to me again. My second thought: thank God I'd decided to rehearse, since blowing up a child, even Andy Tuckerman, on live TV was the sort of disaster from which my career would never recover.

Cautiously I prepared my miniature mill for a second trial, adding fuel to the funnel—a mere teaspoon this time—then inserting the lighted candle. But before I could restore the lid to the paint can, Uncle Wonder's Motorola flared to life, displaying an unstable but intelligible picture: perhaps a feed from an NBC camera, I thought, though more likely, considering the fuzziness of the image, a broadcast struggling to cope with the disconnected rabbit ears. The scanning-gun limned an outlandish life-form suggesting a svelte blue lobster with serrated claws and a grasshopper's rear legs. Its visual system was tripartite—three large eyeballs protruded from its brow on pliant stalks—and its toothless mouth opened and closed along the vertical axis.

"Greetings, Earthling!" shouted the crustacean, a line I'd promised myself I would never use in a *Brock Barton* episode. "Salutations, O Kurt Jastrow! We have converted your television into a pangalactic transceiver! Even as you watch this broadcast, we are hurtling toward you from our home planet, Qualimosa in the Procyon system!"

"I see," I said, suppressing a smirk. Evidently my counterparts at ABC's *Planet Patrol* were playing a practical joke.

A second bipedal lobster entered the shot, as obese as its colleague was skinny. (Stay tuned for Laurel and Hardy in *Two Chumps from Outer Space*.) "We apologize for the murky image! When we talk again on Wednesday, our ship will be closer to Earth and the transmission much clearer!"

"Know this, O Kurt Jastrow!" cried the skinny lobster. "All the brightest people on Qualimosa adore *Uncle Wonder's Attic*! In a galaxy riddled with self-delusion, your program stands as a beacon of scientific enlightenment!"

"I see," I said, trying not to snicker. "I have trouble believing that, of all the programs emanating from Earth, you think mine's the best."

"Truth to tell, Qualimosa's engineers are still calibrating our planet's TV antennas!" the fat lobster explained. "Beyond *Uncle Wonder's Attic*, we have thus far tuned in only *Texaco Star Theater*, hosted by a boisterous comedian who dresses in women's clothes, and *Howdy Doody*, featuring a mentally defective child!"

"Well, if *those* are the choices," I said, "then my show is indeed a beacon of enlightenment."

"We humbly request that, during your Wednesday broadcast, you announce our imminent arrival!" the skinny lobster declared. "Please tell your viewers that, instead of a science experiment, Friday's program will feature an awards ceremony!"

"Harken, O Kurt Jastrow!" the fat lobster demanded. "You will be the first recipient of a trophy forged expressly for those who champion reason in its eternal war with revelation! We mean to visit your attic set and, standing before millions of viewers on Earth and Qualimosa, present you with the Zorningorg Prize!"

"This is a gag, right?" I said. "You're from ABC. Hardy har har."

"A gag, O Kurt Jastrow?" wailed the skinny lobster. "Your hypothesis is false!"

"Hardy har har not!" added the fat lobster. "Behold!"

It really happened. I saw it with my own eyes. The dressmaker's dummy, which normally sat inertly in the corner on a small tripodal stand, began to move. *Clank, clank, clank* went the three wrought-iron feet as they stomped across the attic set. The next thing I knew, the headless automaton had marched past the steamer trunk, circled Uncle Wonder's worktable, and returned to its original position.

"Praised be the gods of logic!" exclaimed the skinny lobster.

"All hail the avatars of doubt!" declared the fat lobster.

And then the Motorola went dark.

Throughout my years as the primary creative force behind *Brock Barton and His Rocket Rangers*, Tuesday morning was always the highlight of the week. Beginning at nine o'clock, NBC's four most gifted dramatists, or so we fancied ourselves, gathered at the Café Utrillo in Washington Square to eat breakfast and critique each other's teleplays. Besides myself, our group included Howard Osborne, who channeled his talents into a Friday night thriller called *Tell Me a Ghost Story*; his comely sister, Connie Osborne, who wrote and produced a Sunday morning religious program called *Not By Bread Alone*; and Sidney Blanchard, who contributed to the prestigious Thursday night anthology series *Catharsis* and also went drinking with Dylan Thomas whenever the celebrated alcoholic poet came to town. We styled ourselves the Underwood Milkers, because we all composed on Underwood typewriters and admired Mr. Thomas's radio play, *Under Milk Wood*, which Sidney had distributed in mimeographed form at the end of our inaugural meeting.

In the sixteen hours that had elapsed between my encounter with the Qualimosans and my arrival at the

Utrillo, I'd decided that my first instinct was correct: my visitors were almost certainly costumed pranksters. As for the Motorola's mysterious resuscitation, they'd probably ignited it via remote control. More difficult to dismiss were the antics of the dressmaker's dummy, but I reasoned that the jokesters could have retrofitted it with springs and pulleys. (I intended to look for the hidden mechanism when I returned to the studio for Wednesday's broadcast.) And so I resolved that during the imminent meeting of the Underwood Milkers I would say nothing about blue bipedal lobsters from outer space.

The agenda for that morning's workshop included an upcoming *Brock Barton* adventure, as well as Connie's latest *Not By Bread Alone* installment. (We'd passed out carbon copies during our previous gathering.) I was not displeased with "The Phantom Asteroid," which found Brock and his crew visiting the gas-giant sector of the solar system to investigate the sudden appearance of a minor planet in orbit between Saturn and Uranus. This strange body turned out to be a spherical machine constructed by the Nonextants, spectral beings to whom the universe belonged "before palpable matter supplanted tangible nothingness as the basic stuff of reality." No sooner did the *Triton*'s crew step onto the machine's surface than Prince Nihil, the sole surviving Nonextant, trapped them "inside a prison constructed ⌐f my ethereal ancestors' nightmares." The last time I'd attempted something this weird—Brock and company spelunking the brain of a Manhattan-sized monster called a Spafongus—the network received enthusiastic letters from about half the children in North America, though we also got a dozen protests from adults accusing us of gratuitous surrealism.

"It doesn't make any sense," said Connie, pushing her "Phantom Asteroid" carbon toward me as if it emitted a disagreeable odor. Among her virtues was an uncanny resemblance, in both voice and appearance, to my favorite Hollywood actress, Jean Arthur. " 'Tangible nothingness'? Really, Kurt, that's a contradiction in terms."

"No, it's science fiction," countered Howard, munching a strip of bacon. "It doesn't *have* to make sense." Of my three fellow Underwood Milkers, only Howard was unstintingly sympathetic to *Brock Barton*, though he seemed incapable of exhibiting this loyalty without making condescending remarks about science fiction *per se*. "If I were a kid encountering Kurt's spectral sphere, I'd think it was swell."

"And if I were a kid encountering Kurt's spectral sphere, I'd switch channels to *Crusader Rabbit*," said Connie, pouring syrup on her French toast.

"Actually, science fiction has to make a *lot* of sense, or else it's just fantasy," I said, passing Connie the July 1953 issue of *Andromeda*. The cover displayed a gleaming disc-shaped spaceship engulfed in a maelstrom of light. This was the third time I'd tried to coax her into reading one of my efforts. "I've got a story in here that extrapolates from Einstein's special theory of relativity."

"The designer made an error," said Connie, pointing to the cover typography, DREAMS OF CHRONOS: A MIND-BENDING NOVELETTE BY KURT JASTROW. "He's implying that this lurid spaceship illustrates your story."

"That lurid spaceship *does* illustrate my story," I said, trying not to sound miffed.

"I wish I could fathom why a man of your intelligence likes that Buck Rogers stuff," said Connie. "I can't begrudge a writer making a living from children's television, but why does he squander the rest of his workday trying to please the editor of *Andromeda*? No thinking person reads it."

"Cousin Greg reads it," Howard informed his sister.

"Case in point," said Connie.

"In pre-Socratic philosophy, Chronos was the person-ification of time," I noted.

"I know," said Connie, eating her French toast.

Of course she knew. Before going to work for NBC, Connie had majored in philosophy at Barnard. I suspected she was some sort of believing Christian—otherwise why was she writing *Not By Bread Alone?*—though she'd once remarked that "in lieu of attending ⁓he volunteered each week at the Saint Francis ⁓ in the Bowery, "ladling out soup for ⁓n though she was "raised Presbyterian

24

and used to think Catholics were scary." Connie idolized the mission's founder and chief administrator, Donna Dain, and she often found herself helping to get out the next issue of Miss Dain's nickel newspaper, the *Catholic Anarchist*.

This is as good a time as any to report that I was madly in love with Connie, although I'd never made any such protestation in her vicinity. As long as she regarded *Andromeda* as a kind of correspondence course for graduates of *Captain Billy's Whiz Bang*, I would garner neither her affection nor her respect.

"Does Cotter Pin *always* have to talk in mechanical-man imagery?" Sidney ate a forkful of eggs benedict, then pressed his "Phantom Asteroid" carbon into my grasp. "I struck out 'Well, I'll be an oscilloscope's uncle' and every other 'Leapin' lug nuts!' I also dumped 'palpable' on the cutting-room floor, likewise 'ethereal.' This is a children's show, for heaven's sake."

We devoted the rest of the meeting to Connie's *Bread Alone* script, "Sitting Shivah for Jesus." First came the usual passage from Schubert's "Ave Maria," played under the off-screen host's standard introduction. *NBC proudly presents stories that dramatize how people of faith, whether residing in ancient Judea or modern America, variously confronting timeless trials and today's tribulations, meet the challenges of daily existence, for men and women live NOT BY BREAD ALONE.* There followed an ingenious and unorthodox drama. Time: the Sunda morning after the crucifixion. Place: the Jerusalem abode of Jesus's best friend, Lazarus. Fade-in on the master of the house and his guests—Joseph, Mary, and their two surviving sons—arrayed around the dining table. They are sitting shivah, meaning "seven," the number of days their formal grieving will last. Through the rear window we glimpse Joseph of Arimathea's sealed crypt, resting place of the Galilean rabbi. Before long the mourners receive a cleansed leper, a cured blind man, and a rehabilitated cripple, who bless the despondent family in the name of the Jesus who healed them. Next, two apostles show up, offering accounts of the Last Supper, and the conversation turns to the dawning doctrine of transubstantiation. In the climax, the stone rolls away from the tomb. Jesus exits, glides toward the house, and appears before his family and beneficiaries, much to their collective and tearful delight. Although the apostles were already committed to spreading the Savior's message of hope and love, this final miracle reinforces their resolve.

"Are you saying Christianity might have flourished even without the resurrection?" Howard asked his sister.

"I'm saying that charity is its own reward," said Connie. "It's not a down payment on eternal life."

"A subversive thesis," said Sidney, delivering his carbon copy to the play's author. "I mean that as a ⁓ my dear. Kindly omit 'My son, my son, are ⁓m the dead?' It's sappy."

⁓onnie with a merry laugh. Were she

and Sidney cultivating a mutual crush? The thought sent my stomach into free fall.

"The whole shivah premise seems self-defeating to me," said Howard. "Jews will think you're appropriating one of their most sacred rituals, and Christians will think you're celebrating Jews."

"That's why God invented television," Connie replied cryptically.

"That's why God invented *unsponsored* television," said Howard. "I can't put anything in *Tell Me a Ghost Story* that violates Procter and Gamble's notions of propriety."

"Can you really get away with Joseph and Mary having their own biological children?" I asked Connie. "The Antidicomarianites will love it, but Cardinal Spellman will throw up."

Once again the *Britannica* had come through for me. Antidicomarianites, literally "opponents of Mary," was a term the Church applied disparagingly to Christians who believed that the siblings of Jesus mentioned in the Gospels were the younger children of Joseph and Mary—an interpretation that made hash of Our Lady's perpetual virginity—as opposed to Joseph's children by a previous marriage, the orthodox view.

Alas, my use of "Antidicomarianites" failed to beguile Connie. She merely told me, testily, "I don't give a fig what Cardinal Spellman thinks. At last report he was in Korea, sprinkling holy water on the U.N. guns."

It occurred to me that neither my *Andromeda* fiction

nor my TV efforts would ever afford me an entrée into Connie Osborne's complicated heart—but there might be a third way. What if I wrote a speculative *Bread Alone* script? What if Connie read the first draft and decided we should develop it together? What if we kicked off our new professional relationship with a dinner date in the Village?

"Connie, there's something I must ask you," I said. "*Not By Bread Alone* is broadcast Sunday mornings at ten o'clock, but isn't your East Coast audience supposed to be in *church* then?"

"True enough," said Connie, taking a final sip of coffee. "Kind of a paradox, I guess."

"Have you considered that most of your viewers might not be very religious?" I said. "Maybe you're preaching to a bunch of doubters."

"Then I've got precisely the audience I want," said Connie, whereupon we Underwood Milkers split the tab and went our separate ways.

2.
LOGICAL POSITIVISTS FROM OUTER SPACE

On Wednesday morning I awoke in thrall to an unfamiliar emotion, which I soon interpreted as the dark side of Uncle Wyatt's cosmic astonishment—a case of cosmic perplexity. Were the Qualimosans truly of extraterrestrial origin? If so, then it behooved me, in the name of interplanetary diplomacy, to use today's installment of *Uncle Wonder's Attic* to herald the forthcoming awards ceremony. But if the whole thing was a hoax, I'd be setting myself up for a mortifying moment, even worse than the time when, unaware that Floyd Cox had neglected to dissolve from the Uncle Wonder attic set to the end title, I began smoking a Chesterfield before three million school children and an apoplectic floor manager.

I needed some advice, and I knew where to get it: 59 West 82nd Street, apartment 3C, where Saul Silver slept, ate, watched TV, brushed his teeth, and edited

Andromeda. Saul would tell me whether or not to take the Qualimosans seriously. Besides, I wanted to pitch him my new idea for a novelette, tentatively titled "Voyage to the Edge of the Universe." I telephoned the great man, woke him up—he kept an erratic schedule—and told him I was anxious to discuss both an embryonic story premise and an odd experience I'd had after yesterday's broadcast. He agreed to meet me at noon.

In those days the adjective "crazy" frequently emerged in conversations concerning Saul Silver, especially when the participants were writers to whom he owed money, but no one could actually defend that diagnosis. Saul was not crazy. He was, rather, agoraphobic—fearful of open spaces—the result of a war trauma he was loath to discuss. By all accounts he hadn't left his apartment in five years, relying on the local bodega to send over his groceries and the U.S. Postal Service to deliver edited manuscripts to the midtown offices of Alpha Enterprises, where publisher Nathan Berkowitz's drones assembled each month's issue of *Andromeda*.

Entering the foyer of Saul's building, I pressed the buzzer for the basement apartment—the electronic connection between 3C and the outside world no longer functioned—thereby summoning his occasional housekeeper, Gladys Everhart, a retired stenographer who supplemented her Social Security income with the monthly $100 stipend Saul paid her for putting up with him. As Gladys and I mounted the stairs, she explained that Mr. Silver was "about to have one of his spells," so she'd soon be leaving on one pretext or another, "since he never likes for me to see him in that state."

The third-floor landing now functioned as an extension of Saul's office, wobbly stacks of *Amazing Stories*, *Astounding*, *Fantastic*, and other *Andromeda* competitors rising from the threadbare Oriental rug. Gladys unlocked the door to 3C—evidently her duties included those of a porter, so that Saul needn't aggravate his agoraphobia by rising to greet visitors—and guided me inside. My heart sank. Illness ascendant, Saul lay sprawled across the sofa, perspiring, rubbing his temples as if to assuage a headache. His fox terrier, Ira, rested on his paunch.

"Morning, Kurt," he said. Despite his condition, or perhaps because of it, the great man always dressed elegantly in a tweed jacket and brown wool tie. "At the moment I'm indisposed, but I'll bounce back."

"You always do," I said, surveying the room. Saul's desk held a Royal typewriter and a swarming mass of manuscripts. The flocked wallpaper displayed a gallery of late twenty-second-century art—rocketships, robots, marching mutants, domed cities—that had once served as *Andromeda* covers. In the far corner two young actors, male and female, filled an Admiral TV set with their anguished conversation: a scene from *Search for Tomorrow*, I figured, or maybe *The Guiding Light* or *As the World Turns.* Why did the names of so many soap operas sound like the titles of science-fiction stories?

Taking a gimp leash in hand, Gladys announced that "somebody needs a walk," a proposition with which the fox terrier obviously agreed. An instant later the housekeeper and Ira sashayed out of the room, the dog's tail wagging like a demented metronome. I elected to get the more difficult task out of the way, saving my edge-of-the-universe novelette for later, so I told Saul all about the Qualimosans' broadcast, their intention to give me the Zorningorg Prize, and the perambulating dressmaker's dummy.

"What the hell kind of a word is 'Zorningorg'?" said Saul. "Sounds like a space monster from some piece of *Amazing Stories* crap. Are these aliens *real*, Kurt?"

"I was hoping you could tell me that."

"What do they look like? Little green men?"

"Large blue lobsters. The dummy trick was pretty convincing."

"Smart money says they're a couple of *schnorrers* in suits, and the dummy was mechanized behind your back. Ah, but smart money isn't always so bright." Saul pulled a handkerchief from his jacket and wiped the sweat from his brow. "Christ on a raft, Kurt, we're in the goddamn *science fiction* business! We're supposed to believe in extraterrestrials, metaterrestrials, überterrestrials, and all such *meshugaas!*"

"So you think I should advertise their appearance?"

"The universe is a far stranger place than we imagine. Yes, Kurt, announce your Qualimosans. If it's all a gag, and they never show up, you'll survive the embarrassment."

The great man's words soothed me. "Thanks, Saul. I'm feeling better." Indeed, part of me would be disappointed if I didn't receive a Zorningorg Prize. Every year the goddamn Ecumenical Outreach Award for Quality Children's Television went to *Planet Patrol*.

"Tell me about this new short story of yours."

"A novelette actually. I call it—"

Saul cut me off with a sudden howl. He spilled off the sofa, dropped to his knees, and crawled across the room. This was not the first time I'd seen him in the throes of an attack, but my pulse still quickened, and my stomach roiled. Reaching the desk, he seized the swivel chair by the seat and sent it scurrying away on its casters. He crept into the empty cavity and curled up like a hibernating bear.

"Anything I can do?" I gasped.

Even as his tissues contracted into a cowering mass of dread, Saul struggled to maintain a professional demeanor. "Guess what? Yesterday's mail brought two fan letters praising your 'Dreams of Chronos.'"

"You seen a doctor yet? He give you a prescription? Should I look in the medicine cabinet?"

"Tell me about your novelette. I don't think there's a pill for this."

"There's always a pill."

"You've got a title, right?"

" 'Voyage to the Edge of the Universe.' "

"There's too much *space* in this city!" Saul ground his teeth, a noise suggesting a chef pulverizing a walnut with mortar and pestle. "At least I don't live on a goddamn prairie. Your novelette, it has a plot?"

"An American astronaut named Adam—"

"Anything but Adam."

"A Russian astronaut, Sergei, sole inhabitant of a manned FTL probe, resolves to venture beyond all imaginable boundaries. Against explicit orders from Washington—I mean Moscow—he guides his probe along our spiral arm of the galaxy—"

"This room is too *big!*"

"And vaults himself into the void. How about we go to the emergency room, Saul? You need a Miltown."

"This will pass! Tell me more!"

"You sure?"

"More!"

"Having exited the Milky Way, Sergei next leaves the galactic cluster behind and eventually reaches the edge of the universe."

"Cushions! On the double!"

"What?

"Cushions! Cushions!"

"Roger! Wilco!"

Frantically I stripped the sofa of its three fat cushions

and jammed them into Saul's cubicle. He embraced the therapeutic pillows as a shipwreck victim might clutch a floating spar.

"You're a prince, Kurt. What happens to Sergei?"

"I'm calling an ambulance."

"What happens to Sergei?!"

"He has entered a zone that defies his powers of rational analysis. The familiar laws of physics no longer apply. He feels like Alice down the rabbit hole."

"Zelda and Zoey!"

"Who?"

"In there!" cried Saul, gesturing toward the coat closet. "Zelda and Zoey!"

I dashed to the closet and pulled back the door, whereupon a pair of rubber love dolls—fully inflated, life-size, all pink flesh and voluptuous parabolas—fell into my arms.

"It's not what you think!" wailed Saul. "I used to have a girlfriend! I intend to get another! I don't use Zelda and Zoey for *that!*"

"Of course not."

As I pressed the pneumatic mannequins into Saul's grasp, tranquility wafted through him, like a cool breeze healing a torrid night. The color returned to his cheeks, and he stopped sweating. He heaved a sigh, hugged his dolls, and asked, "Does Sergei go mad?"

"Not quite, but he now lives in despair—how else would a sane man react to discovering that the triumphant progress of human knowledge has been an illusion? You're looking better."

"The girls have never failed me."

"But then Sergei experiences a revelation. Just as that exquisite system called Newtonian physics operates within a relativistic universe, so does that grand enterprise called experimental science offer intimations of something more glorious still."

"Good twist," said Saul. "Beyond reality. I like it."

"Our hero has broached that blessed state Socrates sought millennia ago. Sergei understands himself to be an ignorant man—and this realization has made him wise."

"Ah, yes, Socrates." Saul relaxed his grip on the love dolls. "What would Kurt Jastrow do without his *Encyclopaedia Britannica*?"

"In the final paragraph Sergei's probe zooms into *terra incognita*, and he is privileged to behold space and time being born before his eyes."

"Can you finish it in two weeks?" said Saul, lurching out of his hidey-hole. Gradually he gained his feet. "I'd like it for the February issue."

"I'll do my best."

"By the way, Sergei can't be Russian. There's a Cold War on. Maybe you hadn't heard? You want Joe McCarthy to come after us? Make him British, and call him Neville."

"Sure thing."

36

"You will excuse me now," said Saul, staggering across the room. "I've got a ton of slush to read, but you can be sure I'll catch your big announcement."

"Wait till four-twenty before tuning in NBC, and you won't have to sit through a *Brock Barton* chapter called 'Fangs of Death.' "

"Get thee to a typewriter, Kurt Jastrow," said Saul, wheeling his chair back into place. "Meet the deadline, and I'll up your salary to four cents a word."

At three o'clock I arrived at Studio One, only to discover that our golden-tonsiled host, Jerry Korngold, had just phoned in sick, a bad case of bronchitis—not a surprise, actually: this was the smoggiest New York November on record. Much to Floyd Cox's distress, nobody in the regular cast was willing to plug the gap. Apparently AFTRA, which I'd never gotten around to joining, forbid its members to sign contracts on the spur of the moment. My initial impulse was to volunteer my own thespian talents—the Writers Guild didn't particularly care if its constituents did impromptu moonlighting on the actors' side of the camera—but then I realized that, at the climax of the episode, I'd have to be in two places at once: the announcer's booth and the attic set.

I suggested recruiting Walter Spalding as our pinch hitter—in his youth he'd played Captain Midnight on the radio—and Floyd agreed, so I went charging down the carpeted hallway toward the executive suites. Mr. Spalding's secretary told me that he, too, was out with bronchitis, so I started back toward Studio One, when who should I meet but Connie Osborne, dressed in a charcoal business suit and carrying a stack of freshly mimeographed *Not By Bread Alone* scripts. I could smell the ink.

"Hi, Kurt—give me a hand with these," she said, dumping half the scripts in my arms. "The read-through can't start till everybody gets a script."

"My show goes on in twenty minutes, and our host is out sick."

"This will only take a sec."

Connie guided me into conference room C, a smoke-filled space dominated by a circular table around which sat the cast of "Sitting Shivah for Jesus." She introduced me to her director, the elderly but energetic Ogden Lynx, who throughout the 1940s had acted in CBS's Sunday-morning religious radio program, *Light Unto the World*.

"My grandchildren are devoted to your show," Ogden told me. Dressed in a loud checked jacket and polka-dot bowtie, he seemed more like a vaudeville comic than a TV director. "I wish *Bread Alone* did as good a job promoting spiritual values as *Brock Barton* does selling Sugar Corn Pops."

"Yesterday Kurt asked me a fascinating question," said Connie. "Why isn't our East Coast audience in church instead of home staring at their TV's?"

"My cousin in the Bronx has it both ways," Ogden replied. "He watches our show and the first half of *Corporal Rex, Wonder Dog of the NYPD*, then walks three blocks and catches an eleven o'clock service at Saint John's Episcopal."

"What profiteth it a man to patronize Rex the Wonder Dog and lose his immortal soul?" I muttered, thus eliciting a scowl from Ogden.

As Connie passed out the scripts, I realized that we might solve our announcer crisis by borrowing one of her performers—maybe ancient Judeans were less beholden to union protocols than Rocket Rangers—but when I asked, she said, "AFTRA won't hear of it, but you can borrow *me*. Mom says I have a chipper Jean Arthur sort of voice."

"Chipper isn't quite right. The role requires gleeful hysteria."

"I can do that, too."

"Aren't you needed here?" I asked, encompassing conference room C with a sweep of my arm.

"Ogden never likes having a producer around when he's working with actors," muttered Connie, "especially if that producer wrote the script."

"Your presence interferes with his creativity?"

"No, it inhibits him from doing capricious last-minute rewrites, one of his principal joys in life."

Seconds later I escorted Connie to Studio One and introduced Floyd Cox to our emergency host.

"Your lines are underscored in red." Floyd handed Connie a script. " 'Fraid I can't give you a contract," he said, ushering her into the announcer's booth. "I'm allowed to hire all the non-union actors I like, so long as I don't pay 'em."

"I'm doing this for the fun of it," said Connie.

"After the flour-mill experiment, cut to a midshot of me," I instructed Floyd. "I'll be making an important announcement."

Two minutes later, receiving her cue, Connie counted down from ten to zero while urging viewers to scramble aboard the *Triton*. "In our last episode," she continued, "the dastardly Argon Drakka arranged for a monstrous python to attack Brock and his crew! Coiling itself around the *Triton*, the serpent suddenly rammed its head through the viewport, threatening Wendy with a razor-sharp tooth! And now we present 'Fangs of Death,' chapter two of 'The Cobra King of Ganymede'!"

As the episode ran its breathless course, I headed for dressing room B, where Trixie Buxton applied my makeup and complained about her husband's drinking. I sprinted back to Studio One. Entering the attic set, I made a beeline for the dressmaker's dummy. I probed the chest, inspected the hips, scrutinized the wrought-iron feet, failing to find any retrofittings that might have animated the thing. Either I'd hallucinated its gyrations, or the dummy had been piloted by alien telekinesis—two theories I found equally disturbing.

Argon Drakka's python did not prosper. No sooner had the creature reared back to strike Wendy than Brock pulled out his blaster and vaporized both fangs, even as Lance Rawlings threw a switch that caused the *Triton*'s hull to overheat and turn the monster into teriyaki. The next sequence required Brock and his crew to traverse Ganymede's harsh terrain toward Drakka's lair. Arriving at the mountain fortress, Cotter Pin deduced that it occupied the site of a dormant volcano. Cut to a commercial: the usual *non sequitur* of Brock savoring Kellogg's Sugar Corn Pops at Galaxy Central. "And remember, kids, it's got the sweetenin' already on it!" Cut back to Ganymede. Acting on Cotter Pin's advice, Brock and Lance dropped a small explosive into the volcano, their goal being to trigger an eruption and thus destroy Drakka's laboratory. Alas, the bomb proved too powerful, causing so prolific a flow of lava—there was nothing Mike Zipser couldn't do with oatmeal—that Brock, Wendy, and Lance found themselves standing in the burning river's path. Fade-out. Cut to Brock doing an Ovaltine commercial. Dissolve to title card, CATARACT OF FIRE.

"Be sure to tune in on Friday for 'Cataract of Fire,' " shouted Connie, "chapter three of 'The Cobra King of Ganymede'!"

Now came *Uncle Wonder's Attic*: an installment that proved mercifully free of catastrophe. True, Andy scratched his scrotum on camera. (Floyd immediately switched to a close-up of the steamer trunk.) True, when sauntering toward my worktable, I tripped over my shoelaces and collided with the dressmaker's dummy. But the flour-mill experiment came off beautifully. When I blew the white powder into the flame, the chemical reaction lifted the paint-can lid three feet into the air—a spectacular but innocuous effect—while the fireball bloomed and vanished in an instant. The set remained intact, Andy was unscathed, and I delivered my big news with aplomb.

"Boys and girls, on Friday we have a special treat for you," I said, facing camera two and resting my palm on the Motorola. "Instead of our usual science experiment, two aliens from Planet Qualimosa will be dropping by to give Uncle Wonder a jim-dandy award, the Zorningorg Prize. I can't tell you much about the Qualimosans, except that they look like saltwater crustaceans and they're very curious about the universe, just like you and me."

"Wow, that's gonna be swell!" said Andy, ad-libbing astutely. "So long, Uncle Wonder! I'm goin' home to try that nifty flour-mill experiment!"

"Great, but remember not to—"

"Not to fill the funnel all the way! Safety first, Uncle Wonder!"

"Safety first!"

Dissolve to end title. Fade-out. Cut to NBC logo.

"So what will happen to Brock, Wendy, and Lance?"

asked Connie, striding into Uncle Wonder's domain, her perky voice ringing across the attic set. "Do they get fricasseed by the lava?"

"But of course," I said with a slanted smile. "It's time kids learned to cope with unhappy endings, don't you think? Terrific performance, Connie. I'm sure Floyd was pleased."

"Walter will get a thousand letters complaining that the show should never be narrated by a woman," said Connie. "Hey, Kurt, what was all that malarkey about a Zorninwhatsis Prize? Don't you think it's boorish to give yourself an award, especially on the air?"

"I'm *not* giving it to myself," I protested, gesturing toward the dormant Motorola. "Evidently I have a following on Planet Qualimosa."

As if on cue, the picture tube glowed to life, revealing the skinny lobster. Just as the aliens had promised, the image was sharper now, and I had no trouble discerning the crustacean's surroundings: the bridge of a spaceship, considerably more textured and detailed that our *Brock Barton* set.

"Greetings, O Kurt Jastrow, in whom we are well pleased!" the skinny lobster declared.

Now the fat lobster appeared on the bridge. "You not only publicized the awards ceremony, you celebrated our philosophy. 'They're very curious about the universe.' Magnificent!"

"Since last we spoke, we have calibrated our onboard

TV antennas to tune in educational programs other than *Uncle Wonder's Attic*," said the skinny lobster. "We are confused, O Kurt Jastrow. Your civilization stands as a bulwark against irrationality, yet we find no scientific substance in the seminars of Liberace or the symposia of Red Skelton."

"It's a cultural crosstalk problem," I said, improvising as cannily as I could. "The substance is there all right, but you have to know where to look."

"Bulwark against irrationality?" said Connie. "What are these clowns talking about?"

"They aren't clowns," I said. "They're benevolent beings from outer space, the whole Michael Rennie bit—at least, I *think* they are."

"This is a gag, right?" said Connie.

"I see you have a friend, O Kurt Jastrow," said the fat lobster.

"Connie Osborne," said my colleague. "I write for TV, too, but you're not about to give me a prize." She turned to me and said, "Fraternity initiation rite?"

"Fraternity rite not, O Connie Osborne," sneered the skinny lobster. "Behold!"

Once again the dummy surged to life. This time, instead of prancing about the set, the thing began spinning like a child's top, then rose toward the studio ceiling and hovered amidst the floodlights.

"Jesus, Kurt, how did you do *that?*" rasped Connie, flabbergasted.

"I didn't do it," I retorted. "The *Qualimosans* did it."

Now the dummy descended—slowly, like a para-trooper—and reassumed its normal place in the attic.

"Jeepers," said Connie.

"We shall arrive on Friday afternoon at four-fifteen, disguised in trench coats and slouch hats," said the skinny lobster. "Tell the security officer to expect us."

"That's cutting it awfully close," I noted.

"Our ship cannot travel faster than the laws of physics allow," said the fat lobster. "After the awards ceremony, we shall visit some of those Manhattan dining establishments about which Lieutenant Lance Rawlings is always reminiscing."

"Do you like seafood?" asked Connie. "I know this great shellfish place on Lexington near Eightieth."

"Connie, please," I said.

"Praised be the gods of logic!" cried the skinny lobster.

"All hail the avatars of doubt!" exclaimed the fat lobster.

Abruptly the Motorola expired, the image contracting to a gleaming pinprick.

"Might we have dinner tonight?" I inquired as the bright speck vanished. "I need to talk to somebody about all this."

"I'll bet you do."

"The Russian Tea Room? Eight o'clock?"

Connie frowned and said, "Tonight I'm having drinks and bar food with Sidney at the White Horse Tavern."

Sidney Blanchard. Criminy. My stomach attempted to digest a stick of rancid butter.

"Dylan Thomas will be there," she added.

"To be honest, I'm often disappointed with Sidney's *Catharsis* scripts."

"I'll suggest he throw in a rocketship next time, or maybe a snake as long as the Holland Tunnel. Here's an idea, Kurt. Come to the Saint Francis House tomorrow night, 90 Ludlow Street, six o'clock. Take the F Train to Delancey. We'll feed the vagrants and talk about your Martians."

"I appreciate that. Hey, Connie, guess what? I've been working on a *Bread Alone* teleplay. Not my strong suit, but I thought I'd give it a shot."

"What's it about?"

"The plot isn't easily summarized," I replied, largely because I wasn't really working on a *Bread Alone* teleplay and therefore had no idea what it was about.

"Toodaloo, O Kurt Jastrow!" declared Connie as, with a bright laugh and a trenchant wink, she handed me her script and strode away.

The next morning I phoned Floyd at his office and told him I wasn't kidding about Friday's installment of *Uncle Wonder's Attic*. He should indeed be prepared to cover a freewheeling awards ceremony featuring two extraterrestrial crustaceans.

"Was this Walter's idea?" asked Floyd. "He'll try anything to goose the ratings."

"Walter knows nothing about it. Connie thinks it's a fraternity stunt. No harm in playing along, I figure."

"Your girlfriend's got a good head on her shoulders," said Floyd. "Jerry's still sick, so I'm putting her back in the announcer's booth."

"She's not my girlfriend."

I spent the afternoon rewriting "The Phantom Asteroid" while trying to think of a viable premise for a Judeo-Christian teleplay. Nothing sprang to mind. Apparently my science-fiction sensibility was inimical to the ethos of religious drama. The immediate future would find me doing my part for the Kellogg's account and the Ovaltine account, but Connie would have to service the God account on her own.

As it happened, my self-diagnosis proved wrong. Riding the F Train toward Delancey Street Station, shielded from November's chill by Uncle Wonder's cardigan, I was visited by an idea for a potentially worthy *Bread Alone* installment, keyed to Jesus's famous observation—Matthew 6:27—that no man had ever lengthened his life by worrying. "Pazuzu Jones, Demon of Regret" would tell of Dr. Felix Olinger, a psychiatrist who makes a diabolical pact. The demon in question agrees to uncouple Felix's psyche from his personal regrets, so that they can no longer cause him mental distress. For his part, Felix must capture each such amputated sorrow, now incarnated as a hideous imp, and cast it down a mine shaft. The bargain soon spins out of control, for our hero keeps encountering missed chances he'd forgotten about. In the end Felix realizes he should have settled for brooding ineffectually on his regrets, just like every other pathetic mortal.

The Saint Francis of Assisi House was an unassuming three-story building near the corner of Broome and Ludlow, the adjacent lot devoted to the stockpiling of wrecked automobiles and the cultivation of givaway vegetables. Hand-lettered signs indicated zones for CABBAGES, BEANS, TOMATOES, and SQUASH, though the produce had long since been harvested. Strikingly attired in a black beret and white wool scarf, Connie appeared on the sidewalk, then ushered me inside. I followed her across a parquet-floored foyer, through a sparsely furnished meeting room, and into the vicinity of a roaring stove. Hell's Kitchen might lie on the far West Side, but Heaven's Kitchen occupied these very premises. I pulled off my coat and sweater, Connie removed her hat and wrap, and we began taking turns stirring an enormous copper kettle abrim with New England clam chowder.

As a somber line of Bowery bums shuffled past, puffing on cigarettes and pushing empty trays along aluminum rails, Connie and two fellow Assisians provided each tramp (mostly men, though I counted seven women) with a bowl of chowder and a hunk of bread. Some of our clients appeared intoxicated, none looked especially healthy, and all were famished. Although I felt like an extra in some creepy Bing Crosby movie about soup-kitchen saints, I believed I understood why Connie chose to spend her spare time this way. "Pazuzu Jones, Demon of Regret" suddenly seemed an embarrassment to me, as spiritually inert as *Texaco Star Theater*.

"Donna Dain invites us to see Christ in every person," she said, "even a scabby wretch whose pants are stained with urine. My analyst thinks I have a savior complex. I tell him there are worse role models than Jesus."

Mirabile dictu, as in a minor-league reenactment of the miracle of the loaves and fishes, our store of victuals was sufficient to feed everyone who showed up that night. After supplying the last tramp with his chowder and bread, we four missionaries—I now considered myself an honorary Assisian—commandeered the remaining portions and adjourned to the basement, a warm but gloomy grotto suffused with cigarette smoke and crammed with vagrants consuming their dinners at dilapidated picnic tables. Slurping sounds filled the air. The far corner evidently functioned as the editorial offices for the *Catholic Anarchist*—conference table, Silex coffee-maker, bank of typewriters, mimeograph machine, back issues papering the walls—and it was here that Connie and I alighted to eat in privacy.

"So how'd it go at the White Horse?" I asked her.

"Horribly," she replied, thereby producing a rush of pleasure in my *Schadenfreude* gland.

"Things not working out between you and Sidney?"

"I'm talking about Dylan Thomas. The man is killing himself. After six straight whiskies, he went to his hotel to lie down. He wanted me to go with him."

"As his nursemaid?"

"His tavern wench."

"Naturally you refused."

"Sidney did that for me," said Connie. "An hour later, Mr. Thomas was back with us. He drank another six, kissed me on the lips, and collapsed. They took him to Saint Vincent's. I expect to read his obituary in tomorrow's *Times*."

" 'Though they go mad, they shall be sane,' " I recited, sipping lukewarm coffee. " 'Though they sink through the sea, they shall rise again. Though lovers be lost, love shall not.' "

" 'And death shall have no dominion.' " Connie smeared butter on her bread. "What shall we discuss first, your Martians or your *Bread Alone* script?"

"I'm afraid I've lost confidence in my script."

"Maybe you can salvage part of it for a *Brock Barton* episode or an *Andromache* story," Connie said with an acerbic grin.

"Andromeda."

"Right." She took a bite of bread. "Let's suppose, for the sake of argument, that these crustaceans are exactly what they say they are. Somewhere beyond our solar system lies a planet of logical positivists."

"Logical positivists?" I offered Connie a perplexed frown, then swallowed a spoonful of chowder.

"Look it up in your *Britannica*. The Vienna Circle of the nineteen-twenties. Verify, verify. No metaphysics allowed. The concept of God is not so much false as incoherent. Eventually the movement reached Cambridge. I hope your Qualimosans aren't typical of alien races. What could be more boring than a galaxy run by Bertrand Russell?"

"A galaxy run by Bishop Sheen?" I suggested. "I hear you'll be announcing tomorrow's show. How about, after the awards ceremony, you join the lobsters and me for our night on the town? I could use an expert in the care and feeding of logical positivists."

"Sure, why not?" said Connie. "Relax, Kurt. They're a couple of frat pledges, probably from Columbia."

"I wonder if Qualimosans die."

"Huh? Everybody dies, Kurt."

"But then you Christians are rewarded with eternal life," I noted.

"I don't know anything about eternal life. Donna says our job is to steal little pieces of Heaven and smuggle them into this mission. As for death, I'll defer to a better writer than myself. 'Do not go gentle into that good night...' "

" 'Old men should burn and rave at close of day,' " I added. " 'Rage, rage, against the dying of the light.' "

"Amen," said Connie.

The following afternoon, fearful that the IRT might break down—it was known to happen—I splurged on a cab, unaware that a labyrinth of interconnected traffic jams lay between the Village and Rockefeller Center. I reached NBC a mere forty minutes before the final chapter of "The Cobra King of Ganymede" would hit the airwaves. Presiding over the front desk was Claude Moffet, a washed-up actor who'd once played Diet Smith on the old *Dick Tracy* radio serial. I told him that, come four-fifteen, two actors wearing trench coats and Mardi Gras lobster costumes would arrive for a guest appearance on *Uncle Wonder's Attic*.

My next stop was dressing room B, where a chattering Trixie transformed me into Uncle Wonder. I hurried to Studio One. Stepping onto the attic set, I realized that, in case the Qualimosans failed to show up, I should have a science experiment ready. I rooted around in the steamer trunk, soon finding the stuff I'd once used to build a Galvanic cell on camera: zinc cathode, copper anode, glass salt-bridge, jars of sulfate solution—plus a flashlight bulb to test the battery's efficacy. Yes, the audience had already seen this demonstration, and, yes, it had nothing to do with today's episode, but I could address both anomalies by declaring that a good experiment was always worth repeating.

Stationed in the announcer's booth, Connie turned

in another fine performance, deftly delivering the recapitulation of Wednesday's cliffhanger, then preparing the audience for chapter three, "Cataract of Fire."

Needless to say, the molten lava did not consume Brock, Wendy, and Lance, who escaped its wrath when Cotter Pin cloaked his friends in an antigravity matrix. The *Triton*'s crew then surveyed the incinerated fortress, seeking proof that they'd dealt a fatal blow to Argon Drakka's python project. Cut to a commercial: Brock at Galaxy Central eating and endorsing Sugar Corn Pops. Cut back to Ganymede. Suddenly Drakka emerged from the ashes, secure within a spacecraft to which he'd tethered his latest creation, a snake-egg the size of a meteor. The evil madman rocketed away, towing the immense spheroid behind him. The *Triton* gave chase. As Drakka approached Earth, his cargo doubled in mass and volume, then trebled, quadrupled, quintupled. Abruptly he cut the egg loose, and it plunged into the Pacific Ocean, cracking open on impact. From the organic capsule an enormous serpent emerged and immediately encircled the planet. (Somehow Mike Zipser persuaded a live python to wrap itself around a huge Rand McNally globe borrowed from the New York Public Library.) "People of Earth!" cried Drakka, broadcasting his threat via his ship's loudspeakers. "Obey me now, or I shall squash your sphere like a tangerine in a chain-mail fist!" At this unnerving juncture, Cotter Pin enacted a daring scheme. Harnessing all his technical prowess, he reversed the Earth's magnetic poles, thus flinging the serpent into deep space. Fade-out. Cut to Brock doing an Ovaltine commercial. Dissolve to title card, THE PHANTOM ASTEROID.

"Join us next week for a brand new adventure, 'The Phantom Asteroid'!" Connie told the audience. "Until then, remember the code of the Rocket Rangers! 'Equality and justice for creatures of all races, colors, creeds, tentacle types, and eyeball arrays'!"

Now Floyd brought up camera three: Uncle Wonder and Andy Tuckerman occupying the attic set as the Motorola displayed the title card, THE PHANTOM ASTEROID. I deactivated the tube, cleared my throat, and glanced at my watch. 4:20 P.M. My crustaceans were five minutes late. Damn.

I decided I'd better resurrect the original script, telling Andy, "I thought our planet was gonna be crushed! What an exciting climax!"

"You can say that again!"

"Hey, Andy, ever wondered how a flashlight battery works?"

"Not lately," said the kid, unhelpfully. "We built one last year, remember?"

"A good experiment is always worth repeating."

From the darkness beyond the attic set, a voice rang out. " 'Equality and justice for creatures of all races, colors, creeds, tentacle types, and eyeball arrays'! A most peculiar imperative!"

I froze. A beguiling scent reached my nostrils. The aliens might look like lobsters, but they smelled like Hershey bars. Lips twitching, feelers trembling, the skinny one ambled onto the attic set, then shrugged off its trench coat and laid its slouch hat atop the Motorola. Facing me squarely, the creature dipped its triclopean head in a deferential gesture.

"O Uncle Wonder, we apologize for our temporal miscalculation. But as Brock Barton once said, 'Better late than never.' "

"Holy mazackers!" exclaimed Andy.

The broadcast TV image had provided no clue to my visitor's scale—it was taller than I'd anticipated: an eight-footer at least. A necklace dangled from the seam between its head and thorax, bearing a pendant resembling the golden statue of Prometheus in Rockefeller Center.

"I am Wulawand, of the gender you call female."

A squeaky-wheeled tea trolley rolled onto the set, pushed by the fat lobster, easily seven feet tall, its slouch hat and trench coat secured in a claw. The conveyance held an object the size of a lampshade, hidden by a gold lamé cloth.

Flinging down its hat and coat, the fat alien bowed before Andy. "Greetings, Master Andrew. How privileged I feel to make your acquaintance. My name is Volavont, of the male gender."

"Am I on camera two or camera three?" asked Wulawand.

"Three," I replied. "Note the tally light."

Wulawand faced the appropriate lens. "Boys and girls of Planet Earth, you cannot imagine how fortunate you are. Back on Qualimosa, a terrible civil war rages between the regiments of reason and the battalions of irrationality."

Andy tugged on my sleeve and whispered, "What's she talking about?"

"Alas, you cannot argue with a religious revelation, children," said Volavont, adding his plump face to the camera-three midshot. "A revelation is always true. Otherwise it would be something else."

"It might be a spittoon, for example," said Wulawand in a caustic tone, "or a stomach pump, or a venereal disease." She emitted a *squonk, squonk, squonk* sound that I took to be the Qualimosan equivalent of laughter.

Fearful that the broadcast was about to take a controversial turn, I pointed to the veiled object and proclaimed, "With profound humility and deep appreciation, I accept this award!"

"But here on Earth revelation has been routed," Wulawand persisted, "thanks in no small measure to Uncle Wonder, who cleanses your minds of metaphysics every Monday, Wednesday, and Friday afternoon!"

"Maybe we should build that battery now," Andy suggested.

"I've never received an award before," I said, whereupon Wulawand seized the gold lamé cloth and pulled it away.

The Zorningorg Prize was as glorious an alien artifact as any *Andromeda* writer might ever hope to contemplate. Five triangular mirrors sloped upward from a pentagonal base to form a pyramidal prism. A rotating, spherical gem commanded the apex, furiously ejecting shafts of crimson, violet, and amber light. As I gazed into the nearest triangle, my mind entered a gallery of kaleidoscopic images that made the expressionist sets in *The Cabinet of Dr. Caligari* seem like two-page spreads from *Better Homes and Gardens*.

"Boys and girls, I wish you all had color TVs!" I exclaimed, vertiginous with rapture. "If only you could see what I see!"

"The Zorningorg Committee hired three of our planet's most renowned artists to design and build your trophy," noted Wulawand.

The longer I stared into the triangle, the more entranced I became. "This honor leaves me speechless! I hope that future installments"—my skull became a radiant chalice—"of *Uncle Wonder's Attic*"—my brain spun on its horizontal axis—"will prove worthy"— I feared I was about to faint—"of the Zorningorg Prize!"

"The visor!" cried Wulawand. "Give him the visor!"

The next thing I knew, Volavont had slipped a set of glass-and-rubber goggles over my head. (Though designed for three eyes, they readily shielded my two.) Beyond the border of the attic set, our floor manager frantically waved his hand in a circle. We were out of time. I must wrap it up.

"See you next Monday, kids!" I cried.

Dissolve to end title. Fade-out. Cut to NBC logo.

Intoxicated by my prize, I collapsed on the floor, and everything went black.

I awoke on my back, stretched across a couch, Connie and Floyd leaning over me wearing expressions of solicitous alarm. Haltingly I sat up and assessed my situation. My goggles were gone, likewise my fake beard and eyebrows. I'd been carried to conference room C. Wrapped in the gold cloth, the Zorningorg Prize loomed beside me on its tea trolley. Andy sat in the far corner, experimenting with a yo-yo. Wulawand and Volavont were nowhere to be seen.

"Try some of this," said Connie, proffering a glass of brown milk. She was beguilingly attired in a silky maroon blouse, its buttons obscured by ruffles.

I took a swallow and licked my lips. Ovaltine was in fact a tasty product. "I'm okay now. Really. Where are the Qualimosans?"

"Back in the shuttle that brought them from their orbiting ship," said Connie. "They're getting you an elixir."

"Isn't the shuttle attracting a lot of attention?" I asked, climbing off the couch.

"Our visitors have mastered a technique called sub-molecular shapeshifting. They've replaced the Rockefeller Center statue of Prometheus with a duplicate that happens to be their shuttle."

"What about the *real* statue?" I asked.

"They shrank it," said Connie. "Did you notice that pendant hanging from Wulawand's neck?"

"Good heavens, you're talking like they're genuine extraterrestrials," said a baffled Floyd.

"The jury's still out," said Connie. "They might be big bruisers in costumes, or they might be the real thing."

"Of *course* they're big bruisers in costumes," said Floyd. "This is a television network. We attract starving actors like Charles Atlas draws ninety-pound weaklings."

Just then both Qualimosans scuttled into the room, dressed in their trench coats and slouch hats, Wulawand fingering her pendant, Volavont clutching a green vial presumably containing the elixir.

"I won't be needing that," I said, pointing to the potion, even as I wondered whether it might cure Saul's agoraphobia.

"O Kurt Jastrow, how marvelous to see you on your feet," said Wulawand. "Volavont and I apologize for not giving you the visor before awarding you the trophy."

"You fellas are the best goddamn Martian act I've ever seen," said Floyd. "If you like, I'll arrange an audition with Mr. Spalding. You ought to have your own god-damn show."

"Mr. Cox, you shouldn't swear in front of the boy," said Connie.

"I've got goddamn sensitive ears," said Andy.

"We are not an act," Wulawand averred.

"I'll also take you to see Peggy Hipple, head of wardrobe," said Floyd. "She'll be bowled over by those suits."

"They are not suits," Volavont insisted.

"Please excuse us, O Floyd Cox," said Wulawand. "We have an urgent matter to discuss with Mr. Jastrow and Miss Osborne. You must leave, too, Master Andrew."

Floyd shrugged and started away. "A word of advice," he told the Qualimosans. "When somebody offers to introduce you to a major TV producer, if behooves you to show a little gratitude."

The director left in a huff, Andy following close behind.

"O Kurt Jastrow," wailed Wulawand, "a lamentable matter has come to our attention. While heading toward our shuttle to obtain the elixir, we found ourselves in the vicinity of Studio Two, where we eavesdropped on a rehearsal for an imminent installment of *Not By Bread Alone*."

"The title is 'Sitting Shivah for Jesus,' " Volavont said, then proceeded to quote the standard introduction. " 'NBC proudly presents stories that dramatize how people of faith, whether residing in ancient Judea or modern America, variously confronting timeless trials and today's tribulations, meet the challenges of daily existence, for men and women live *not by bread alone.*' "

"We are grieved to report that certain writers and actors at this network are in the grip of superstition," said Wulawand. "In 'Sitting Shivah,' the characters speak of lepers experiencing miracle cures, bread becoming meat, and crucified rabble-rousers cheating death."

Connie and I exchanged glances of mutual bewilderment and tacit understanding: don't contradict the lobsters—at least, not yet.

"By consulting our shuttle's onboard computer," said Wulawand, "we learned that *Not By Bread Alone* is broadcast regularly to television receivers throughout the continental United States. A secret society, two million strong, watches the program every Sunday morning, beginning at ten o'clock Eastern Standard Time."

"Respectable ratings," I said.

"Do not despair, O Kurt Jastrow," said Wulawand. "Take heart, O Connie Osborne. Follow us back to Studio One, where we shall demonstrate a quick and simple antidote to televised irrationality."

"An antidote we shall provide free of charge," added Volavont. "Praised be the gods of logic!"

"Logic is a girl's best friend," said Connie, grimacing.

"Couldn't get through the day without it," I said, biting my tongue.

Taking hold of my veiled trophy, I headed for the door, distressed by my certainty that a Qualimosan antidote to televised irrationality would have nothing to recommend it.

Ten minutes later Connie and I stood together in Uncle Wonder's attic. The lights were dark, the cameras inactive, the Motorola's tubes inert. After setting my award beside the steamer trunk, I fixed on the dressmaker's dummy, which now seemed monstrous to me, the vanguard of an alien invasion.

"Qualimosa's engineers strive incessantly to keep the torch of reason burning," said Wulawand. "Recently they discovered that the scanning-gun of an ordinary cathode-ray tube can be appropriated to exterminate viewers of any philosophically problematic narrative borne by the electromagnetic spectrum."

In all my years of reading science fiction, I'd never encountered a sentence quite like that one. "You're not serious," I said, feeling faint for the second time that day.

"Exterminate them?" said Connie through clenched teeth.

"If you prefer, we shall annihilate them," said Wulawand. "Contrariwise, we could perpetrate a massacre."

From her trench coat the female lobster withdrew two devices, the first suggesting a swivel-necked vegetable peeler, the second a dispenser of cellophane tape. She attached the peeler, blade pointed downward, to one of the rabbit ears, then switched on the Motorola. Gradually the picture tube warmed up. Visual static danced across the glass. Wulawand changed channels. More static.

"You won't get a strong signal," I explained. "That monitor's wired to receive title cards only."

"So the rabbit ears are merely decorative?" said the female crustacean. "We can fix that."

Wulawand nonchalantly pulled a screwdriver-like device from her coat, detached the spade lugs securing the cable to the Motorola, and connected the rabbit ears, thereby causing the Cisco Kid to gallop across the screen. The male Qualimosan, meanwhile, waded into the bric-a-brac and retrieved the dressmaker's dummy. Wulawand changed channels. Static. Again she rotated the dial. *The Howdy Doody Show* popped onto the tube.

"Before we sought you out in conference room C, I used this transceiver to contact Yaxquid, the navigator of our orbiting spaceship." From beneath her carapace Wulawand produced an object suggesting a green ocarina. "Acting on my orders, he placed our X-13 death-ray projector on standby alert. Come Sunday morning, shortly after the *Bread Alone* cult has gathered around their television sets—"

"Somewhere in the temporal vicinity of ten minutes after ten," interrupted Volavont.

"After the cult has gathered," Wulawand continued, "I shall call Yaxquid again, telling him to piggyback the death-ray onto the carrier wave of every NBC affiliate station in North America."

"An instant later," said Volavont, "your planet will be cleansed of all two million irrationalists."

"I see," I said, hyperventilating.

"My, my," gasped Connie, pale as cottage cheese.

"If for some reason Yaxquid hasn't heard from me by twenty minutes after ten," said Wulawand, "the death-ray will fire automatically."

"What a technologically advanced civilization you are," I said, squeezing both fists: heartless aliens, promiscuous death-rays, casual slaughter—this was science fiction at its worst.

"For the present demonstration, the X-13 is not needed," said Wulawand, pointing to the vegetable peeler. "We shall use this compact model, the X-2. Behold!"

Leaning toward the rabbit ears, Wulawand rotated the axis of the peeler. The device glowed violet and begin whining like a theremin. An instant later a rapier of light shot from Howdy Doody's left eye and skewered the dummy, setting it on fire.

"Jesus!" cried Connie.

"Good Lord!" I yelled.

Wulawand touched the handle of the peeler, causing the death-ray to vanish and the whine to fade, while Connie and I pulled a quilt from the steamer trunk and wrapped it around the burning dummy, smothering the flames. We looked into each other's frightened eyes: somehow we must outfox these homicidal lobsters— though just then they seemed to hold all the aces.

"This is all very impressive," I said as the glimmer of an idea illuminated a normally obscure region of my brain, "but I'm afraid you misinterpreted that 'Sitting Shivah' rehearsal."

"Misinterpreted, exactly," Connie chimed in, obviously wondering what I would say next, which was a mystery to me as well.

"In point of fact, *Not By Bread Alone* is a *satiric* program," I asserted. "It *mocks* belief in the supernatural."

"We didn't see much mockery today," said Volavont. "Against all reason, a political dissident returned from the dead."

"What you witnessed was the first of six or seven rehearsals," I said, improvising madly. "The actors always work with the irrational material *first,* so they'll be able to deliver it with conviction. The most valuable satire does not burn straw men. It melts mighty icons."

"That makes sense," Volavont conceded.

"Even a *child* can burn a straw man," added Connie.

Striding toward the rabbit ears, I unfastened the X-2, then handed it to the skinny lobster. "So you see, Wulawand, you won't be needing this after all."

"Not so fast, O Kurt Jastrow! How do we know that what you say is true?"

"Would Uncle Wonder tell a lie?"

A vertical grimace claimed Wulawand's face, and her invertebrate body assumed a skeptical pose. "Harken to our terms. On Sunday morning, in deference to your assertion concerning *Not By Bread Alone*, Volavont and I shall tune in the broadcast on some TV or other, while our navigator monitors the show from our spaceship. If 'Sitting Shivah' indeed proves satiric, we shall contact Yaxquid at ten minutes after ten as planned." Again the crustacean flashed her ocarina. "Our message will be simple: we were mistaken about the irrationality cult— deactivate the X-13."

"But if the program is in fact purveying metaphysical drivel, Wulawand will order Yaxquid to call down the death-ray," said Volavont. "Fair enough?"

"Fair enough," I said, raging internally.

"Of course, we must avoid getting skewered by our own brochette." Wulawand crept toward the steamer trunk and yanked the gold cloth from my award. "After Volavont and I suspend this impervious veil in front of the picture tube, we shall be able to watch the program without misadventure."

"Such precautions won't be necessary," I insisted. "Last year *Not By Bread Alone* won the Voltaire Award for Theological Impertinence."

"I can hardly wait to see the icons melt," said Volavont.

He wouldn't have to wait long. Connie and I had only forty hours to write, cast, and rehearse the new teleplay.

"As the 'Sitting Shivah' production evolves, some characters will be dropped altogether while new parts are added for other NBC actors," I said. "Brock Barton and his crew sometimes make guest appearances on *Not By Bread Alone*."

"They do?" muttered Connie.

"The final version will be as impious as a turd in a baptismal font," I promised the lobsters.

"Sacrilege on stilts," added Connie, wincing. She wasn't going to enjoy turning her elegant teleplay into a farce, not one little bit. "A jamboree of blasphemy. A circus of irreverence."

"I love circuses," said Volavont. "By the way, I'm famished."

"Myself as well," said Wulawand, tucking the ray-proof cloth into her carapace. "Let us now patronize three or four of those swank restaurants for which Manhattan is famous."

The thought of spending the evening explaining trench-coated crustaceans to maître d's and Diners Club members filled me with apprehension. "You know what you two *really* need?" I said. "A home-cooked meal, that's what." Although the cuisine at 378 Bleecker Street, apartment 4R, was spartan, I always kept my favorite prepackaged food on hand. "Once you get a taste of Kraft macaroni and cheese, you'll want to take *tons* of it back with you."

"It appears that we are all friends again," said Wulawand.

"O Kurt Jastrow, I wish we could give you a Zorningorg Prize every day of the year," said Volavont.

I marched up to the Motorola and flipped off the tube, sending Howdy Doody into oblivion.

3.
COFFEE WITH CHRIST AT CHOCK FULL O' NUTS

Connie and I agreed that, as a first step in foiling the Qualimosans, I should secretly contact my roommates and prepare them for two guests whose resemblance to immense blue bipedal lobsters was best accorded an extraterrestrial interpretation. A Rexall drugstore on 54th Street supplied the necessary pay telephone. Connie contributed the nickel. Lenny answered on the first ring. Probably owing to his bohemian sensibility, he greeted my narrative of alien invasion with minimal skepticism, and he seemed to accept the logic of my argument: only a last-minute *Not By Bread Alone* rewrite could save two million innocent television viewers from an X-13 death-ray.

"I always knew the flying-saucer people were out there, and sooner or later they'd land on Earth," said Lenny. "But I never imagined they'd be so antagonistic to God."

"They're logical positivists, or so Connie tells me."

"Eliot's going to have a lot of trouble with this," said

Lenny, "especially their plan to throw all those Christians to the lions."

"The rule for tonight's visit is simple," I said. "No metaphysics. Take down Eliot's poster of the Buddha. Hide your copy of the Upanishads. Make no mention of Cardinal Spellman, the Pope, or any other Christian celebrity. If you can't say something nice about logical positivism, say nothing at all."

"Gotcha."

"Now here's a tougher assignment. I suspect that Qualimosans never sleep, so we'll need some way to amuse them while Connie and I sneak off and give her script a makeover. Maybe you could show our guests a couple of movies on that projector you got when the *New Yorker* commissioned 'The Celluloid Rebels.'"

"The piece was called 'The Celluloid Insurgents,' and I sold it to the *Brooklynite*," Lenny corrected me. "I'll telephone my cousin Marvin in Queens. Last year he bought up a lot of Army-surplus horror movies—you know, the sort of 16mm prints the G.I.s got to see when they weren't killing Nazis. I'll bet your flying-saucer people would think Bela Lugosi is the bug's nuts."

"Lugosi? Are you kidding? The Qualimosans are allergic to supernaturalist narratives."

"We'll skip Lugosi's vampires and confine the festival to his mad doctors. A romantic but basically level-headed lot, all fiercely committed to the scientific worldview."

"I don't like it."

"You got a better idea?"

"No."

"Bye, Kurt. See you soon."

At first the Yellow Cab driver I flagged down was reluctant to accept, along with two seemingly normal fares, a pair of trench-coated exhibitionists who thought it was still Halloween, but then I waved a twenty-dollar bill in his face, saying he could keep the change. "For twenty bucks, I don't care if your fabulous fairyland costume party is in frigging Connecticut," said the cabbie, a mustachioed man whose hackney license identified him as Rocco Spinelli. "Lemme guess—I'm takin' you to Greenwich Village."

"Bull's-eye," I said.

"Chocolate cologne!" said the cabbie. "What will you drag queens think of next?"

"Drive on, O Rocco Spinelli!" ordered Wulawand.

"And remember, our death-ray is not just for irrationalists," Volavont added. "Sometimes we set our sights on sarcastic vertebrates."

We passed the next half-hour jammed together in the taxi, Connie and the lobsters riding in the back seat, myself ensconced beside the driver, the Zorningorg Prize, now cloaked in Uncle Wonder's cardigan sweater, balanced on my lap. Connie took the opportunity to chat with Wulawand and Volavont. Both crustaceans were delighted to learn that, in the lexicon of Western academic philosophy, they were logical positivists.

Elaborating, Connie breezily declared that this world-view overlapped considerably with "the reigning ethos of Planet Earth, secular humanism."

"At my *alma mater,* Barnard College, anyone who questions the principle of empirical verification is called a twaddle coddler," she insisted. "Your *Weltanschauung* also partakes of the atomism favored by the Greek philosophers Democritus and Epicurus."

"Marvelous," said Wulawand.

"I love this planet," said Volavont.

"Logical positivism has its critics, of course," said Connie. "This system must consign ethics to the sphere of arbitrary emotivism. It's difficult to get from 'is' to 'ought' using only linguistic analysis."

"Ethics?" said Wulawand. "What is ethics?"

"Nothing you need worry about," I piped up from the front seat, fearful that Connie's answer would antagonize the lobsters. "Miss Osborne's point is that almost every-one on our world thinks logical positivism is just as swell as secular humanism."

"As I told your audience this afternoon, Qualimosa is in the throes of a civil war," said Wulawand. "The first shots were fired two hundred years ago, after a clever young scientist, Professor Squatront, advanced a persuasive theory concerning the origin of our planet's premier species—and all its other life-forms as well."

"Squatront argued that we could account for ourselves entirely through materialist evolutionary processes," said

Volavont. "Narratives of special creation by a Supreme Being were tales for children."

"I'm thankful that no such controversy ever emerged here on Earth," said Connie.

"You don't know how lucky you are," said Wulawand.

Darkness had fallen by the time we reached 378 Bleecker Street. Squeezing the award against my chest, I led Connie and the lobsters up the stairs to the fourth floor landing, trying to tamp down my fear that, outraged by the Qualimosans' murderous intentions, my roommates would treat them with the same caliber of hostility Joe McCarthy accorded Communists.

I needn't have worried. Lenny welcomed Wulawand and Volavont magnanimously, adding even a dash of the cavalier, as if extraterrestrial dinner guests were just another interesting feature of life in the big city. Eliot, too, had apparently decided to fête our visitors for now and reckon with their sociopathy later. After ascertaining from Wulawand that feeler-stroking constituted the standard Qualimosan salutation, he greeted both aliens in this manner, then offered them *vino* from a wicker-wrapped Chianti bottle he'd been "saving for a special occasion," though obviously not *this* special occasion.

"Fermented juice from a fruit we call grapes," Eliot explained to the lobsters.

"It sounds exquisite," said Wulawand.

"Please decant the beverage in question," said Volavont.

"None for me, thanks," said Connie.

"I'm supposed to pound out a script tonight," I said, shaking my head.

As Eliot uncorked the Chianti, Lenny curled an arm around my neck and whispered, "An emergency Bela Lugosi delivery is on the way."

"You'll get a medal for this," I said.

Eliot filled four glasses with Chianti, and the invertebrates immediately started guzzling. Connie and I repaired to the kitchen, where I secured my cardigan-covered trophy atop the refrigerator, snugging it between the cathedral radio and the Hasbro Toy Company's windup tinplate version of Cotter Pin. Speaking *sotto voce*, we simultaneously prepared dinner and plotted our strategy.

"With any luck, we'll be able to meet with half your 'Sitting Shivah' actors tomorrow," I told Connie, filling a saucepan with tap water, "plus four or five *Brock Barton* regulars."

"My top priority is relieving Ogden of his directorial duties," she said. "As the show's producer, I can bounce him from any episode. I won't enjoy firing him, but if he ends up in the control room Sunday morning, he's bound to cause trouble."

"He can't abide sacrilege?" I asked

Connie nodded and said, "I'm not wild about it either, but I'll do anything to thwart your horrid Martians."

"Maybe Ogden will be equally flexible," I suggested.

"Show him the charred dummy, show him your trophy—he'll still think it's all a joke at the expense of the Lutheran Church."

I lit the stove and set the saucepan on the open flame. "So who's going to direct this clambake?"

"Me, unless you've got a better idea."

"You'll be terrific," I said. "I see a Zorningorg Prize in your future."

For the next five minutes we stared at the water, waiting for it to boil.

"Then there's the problem of the script itself," said Connie.

"What script?"

"That's the problem."

"The evening is young," I said. "Lenny has a scheme for keeping the Qualimosans distracted while you and I slip away to some garret or other. It involves a cache of old horror movies."

"I'm not following you," said Connie as a constellation of bubbles rose to the water's surface.

"Lenny feels pretty confident."

"I suggest we write our script at the Saint Francis House." Connie opened a box of Kraft macaroni, removed the cheese envelope, and dumped the remaining contents in the boiling water. "Donna never turns off the heat, and we can probably use the *Catholic Anarchist* mimeo machine."

"Don't worry about the sacrilege, Connie." I stirred the macaroni with a wooden spoon, the pasta bits swirling like motes in a nebula. "God will understand. I hear he's a pragmatist at heart, very keen on William James."

Forty minutes later the six of us sat down to a meal of bread, butter, and cheese-flavored macaroni, three boxes' worth. Wulawand and Volavont derived as much pleasure from playing with their food as eating it. (They especially enjoyed blowing into the hollow pasta segments to create high-pitched whistles.) When the crustaceans declared that they found the main course scrumptious, I took this assessment at face value, though their satisfaction was doubtless enhanced by the second bottle of Chianti, which Lenny had found in our pantry behind a pyramid of Campbell's tomato-soup cans.

"Don't think me rude if I go to bed soon," said Eliot, yawning. "Today I had four absolutely *grueling* auditions."

I turned to Wulawand and said, "You're welcome to toss some blankets and mattress pads on the floor—or will you be sleeping in your shuttle tonight?"

"What is sleeping?" she asked.

"A lapse in rational consciousness," I replied.

"Ah, you mean *religion,*" said Volavont, emitting the

squonk, squonk, squonk noise by which Qualimosans expressed amusement.

"Very clever," I said with a forced guffaw as Connie rolled her eyes.

When Eliot realized we had no dessert on hand, he volunteered to fetch some ice cream from the corner bodega. Before he left, I quietly instructed him to return with vanilla and strawberry only. (Because our guests smelled like chocolate, I explained, that flavor might smack of cannibalism.) No sooner had Eliot departed than Lenny marched to the hall closet and pulled out his Bell & Howell Filmosound projector. His present *Brooklynite* assignment, he explained, concerned Bela Lugosi, "the king of anti-metaphysics melodramas." Because the Hollywood legend's latest low-budget vehicle, *The Phantom of Flatbush*, was set largely in Brooklyn, Lenny's editors had decided the magazine should do a 10,000-word Lugosi feature, complete with a sympathetic review of the new movie, a biographical sketch, and an impressionistic survey of the Hungarian actor's greatest performances.

"The only way I can meet the deadline is to stay up all night watching my cousin Marvin's collection of Lugosi classics," Lenny told the lobsters. "Please join me. These entertainments celebrate logical positivism at its finest. *Murders in the Rue Morgue* finds Lugosi playing Dr. Mirakle, whose scientific curiosity can be satisfied only by infusing a virgin with an orangutan's blood, his goal being to create a mate for his talking sideshow ape, Erik."

If I correctly recalled the *Daily Variety* coverage, *The Phantom of Flatbush* had indeed opened recently—on Halloween, appropriately, and to sluggish business, predictably. But Lenny had certainly received no Lugosi assignment from the *Brooklynite*. My journalist roommate, God bless him, was prevaricating for the greater good.

Within fifteen minutes of Eliot's return from the bodega, the ice cream had disappeared, most of it into alien alimentary canals, Wulawand expressing a preference for the vanilla, Volavont favoring the strawberry. But they were utterly ecstatic about the candy Eliot had impulsively purchased. Consuming their 3 Musketeers bars, the crustaceans declared that nougat was as delectable as logic.

Not long after our guests had savored their final morsels of Athos, Porthos, and Aramis—the chocolate component evidently gave them no offense—I announced that Connie and I were facing a deadline as severe as Lenny's. We'd be spending the rest of the evening back at NBC, collaborating on a teleplay.

"We are not familiar with Miss Osborne's TV credits," said Wulawand.

"My pen is for hire to the highest bidder," said Connie. "Sometimes they pay me to rehabilitate one of Kurt's scripts."

"But not often," I said.

"I also do crime thrillers, soap operas, westerns, and even religious satires of the sort featured on *Not By Bread Alone*," said Connie.

Lenny headed for the kitchen, declaring that he planned to make a batch of Quickie-Bang popcorn for the imminent Lugosi festival. As the staccato reports of his culinary efforts filled the air, *pop, pop, pop, pop,* I slipped into my bedroom, hoping to find my *NBC Radio and Television Personnel Directory* as well as Connie's original "Sitting Shivah for Jesus" script. Upon locating both documents—the directory lay under my bed like an orphan shoe, the teleplay was sandwiched between the July and August issues of *Andromeda*—I secured them in a satchel and returned in time to see Lenny slice open an aluminum-foil dome rising from the Quickie-Bang skillet.

"Positivism always goes better with popcorn," he said, pouring the steaming kernels into a wooden salad bowl.

Just then a buzzing noise resounded throughout the apartment. Lenny pushed the intercom button and leaned toward the microphone. "That you, Marvin?"

"You owe me three bucks for the taxi," came the electronically enhanced voice of Lenny's cousin, crackling up from the front stoop. "I suggest we start with *The Black Cat*. It's Lugosi's best performance after Ygor."

"*The Black Cat*?" said Wulawand. "That does not

sound like a rationalist drama to me. In our pangalactic travels Volavont and I have noticed that black domesticated tetrapods typically occasion crude superstitions."

"Give it a chance," said Lenny, his finger still on the button. "In the final reel, Lugosi's Dr. Werdegast shuts down a foolish devil-worshiping cult by skinning the leader alive."

Once again Marvin's voice poured from the speaker. "Somebody get the hell down here and help me with these goddamn film cans!"

As Lenny and Eliot headed for the stairwell, Volavont rested a claw on my shoulder and said, "*The Black Cat* must be one of your favorite motion pictures."

"Oh, I simply *adore* it," I said, even though I'd never seen the thing. "I would screen the climax on *Uncle Wonder's Attic*, but the children might find it too intense."

"You are a soft-hearted creature, O Kurt Jastrow," said Wulawand. "Be careful. One never knows down what dark valleys tenderness may lead."

Before Connie and I left the apartment that night, Lenny engaged in an act of chivalry. Having judged her cloth coat inadequate to the bitter November wind, he lent Connie his black leather motorcycle jacket. The garment looked smashing on her, though in my lovelorn state I would have appreciated her in a potato sack. Still huffing and puffing from the exertion of hauling his share of Lugosi films up four flights of stairs, Lenny's cousin—a pleasant if gnomish young man—lost no time feeding her a line from *The Wild One*.

"What are you rebelling against, Johnny?" asked Marvin.

"Whaddaya got?" Connie replied, doing a passable Brando.

Despite my colleague's assurances that all four *Catholic Anarchist* typewriters were functional, I decided to bring my own machine along. Shortly after nine o'clock we hailed a cab, then traveled from the Village to the Bowery, the Underwood sitting on my lap as I'd earlier borne my Zorningorg Prize. Arriving at the Saint Francis House, we descended to the basement and made our way to the newspaper office through the hobos, winos, and lost souls, some of them sleeping on the floor, others eating hot chili at the picnic tables, still others watching *Our Miss Brooks* on CBS. I soon apprehended, to my immense relief, that both telephones were free, likewise the mimeo machine.

Connie draped the back of a chair in Lenny's motor-cycle jacket and yanked the NBC personnel directory from my satchel. "I need to get the worst part over with. Wish I could talk to my analyst first, but he never gives advice after hours."

She dialed Ogden Lynx's number, pausing a full second between digits, then pointed toward the second telephone and invited me to eavesdrop.

"Hello, Ogden. Connie here. Listen, something's come up. My 'Sitting Shivah' script—I'm just not happy with it."

"Not happy?" said Ogden. "What're you talking about?"

"The tone's all wrong. I was trying for poignancy, but it came out sentimental. I'll never forgive myself if it's broadcast on Sunday."

"You wrote a masterpiece," Ogden protested. "It made me cry."

"It made me cry, too, but for different reasons. The new draft is almost finished. Fewer characters, more eschatological resonance. Tomorrow I'll track down the actors—the ones I still need—and give 'em their new lines."

"AFTRA will never abide an emergency rehearsal—not unless we pay everybody overtime," said Ogden, "and you know Walter won't stand for that."

"Then we'll have to make do without a rehearsal."

"Have you lost your mind?"

"No, I've lost faith in my script."

"When do I get to see the rewrite? Can you drop it off tonight?"

"That's the thing, Ogden. You won't be directing this episode. I've got some stylistic flourishes in mind, the sort of stuff I always put in the stage directions and you always ignore."

"Connie, this is madness. Come over here right now, and we'll pray together."

"No time for that. Enjoy your day off. Next week I'll show you a brand new script, 'The Three Wishes of Jenny O'Keefe.' Buckets of tears. Bye-bye."

"No!"

Connie restored the handset to its cradle. "I never want to fire anybody again."

"You acquitted yourself well," I said. "Your analyst would've been proud of you."

We plugged in the Silex, brewed some coffee, and threw ourselves into our first task, chasing down the cast of "Sitting Shivah" and the crew of the space schooner *Triton*. Constrained by the clock—we still had a half-hour teleplay to write—we could offer each actor only a thumbnail account of the crisis: invading rationalists, impending massacre, ethically essential rewrite. After much to-and-froing, back-and-forthing, begging, wheedling, entreating, and cajoling, our Saturday schedule was fixed.

At noon we would go to the Chock Full O' Nuts in Herald Square and meet with Jesus Christ—that is, we'd drink coffee with stage, screen, and picture-tube stalwart Ezra Heifetz—along with Calder Bolling, who played Cotter Pin, and Joel Seddok, a former wrestling champion who regularly zipped himself into Sylvester Simian's gorilla costume. Come 6:00 P.M. our itinerary would take us to the White Horse Tavern, where Hollis Wright, the *Triton*'s fearless captain, would receive his new script, likewise Jimmy Breeze, who brought such brio to the role of Ducky Malloy, plus the actors Ogden had cast as the apostle Peter, the cleansed leper, and the not-quite-Virgin Mary. As for the other characters who might have graced the rewrite, we reluctantly consigned them to oblivion, for the corresponding actors had either failed to answer the phone (the ingénue who incarnated Wendy Evans), pleaded unbreakable commitments (the *alter egos* of the cured blind man, the rehabilitated cripple, and Lieutenant Rawlings), or simply refused to countenance a parody of "Sitting Shivah" on the off-chance it might deter an extraterrestrial death-ray (the response we received from the talent contracted to play Lazarus, Joseph, the apostle Matthew, and Jesus's non-divine brothers).

"And now we conjure the ghosts of Bertrand Russell and Mark Twain," said Connie, pointing to my Underwood. "I'd much rather be feeding soup to bums."

Being the better typist, I volunteered to transcribe the evening's brainstorms. For the next four hours, like auctioneers conducting parallel fire sales, Connie and I shouted out potential dialogue, stage directions, and plot twists, even as I committed our most viable notions to paper. I'd never collaborated on a writing project before, and I happily observed that the process got my creative juices flowing. My partner, I sensed, was likewise galvanized—or would have been were our goal not to make her divine Creator look ridiculous.

We decided to lead with the ace of trumps: an impudent reworking of the announcer's opening pitch, so that it now read, "NBC proudly presents stories alerting viewers to the ways that people of faith, whether living in ancient Judea or modern America, have impoverished their intellects with supernatural explanations of reality, for a mind cannot thrive on self-delusion any more than a body can live by bread alone. Stay tuned for 'The Madonna and the Starship'!"

> *Absently stroking the fruit bowl on Lazarus's dining table, sitting shivah alone, Mary faces the camera and tells the audience how on Friday her firstborn son, a rabbi given to spreading incendiary political ideas, was tortured and killed by the Romans. Alas, no one came to see her on Saturday, the Sabbath, but she hopes that a comforter or two might appear this morning.*
>
> *No sooner has Mary voiced her desire than Peter enters, explaining that he and Matthew have conspired to save Jesus's life. The nexus of their plot is the sponge from which the rabbi drank during his crucifixion. Although the Roman executioners believed the sponge held mere vinegar, it actually contained an opiate that reliably produces the symptoms of*

death. And so it happened that Jesus was removed from the cross while his heart still beat, taken to Joseph of Arimathea's crypt, and interred alive.

Cut to the rear window with its view of the sealed tomb. The stone rotates free of the portal. Much to Mary's wonderment, her son comes forth, staggers toward Lazarus's house, and enters the dining room. Having been driven mad by his ordeal of premature burial, Jesus insists that he is none other than God himself.

Mary is taken aback by her son's lunacy, but before she can articulate her bewilderment, Brock Barton, Ducky Malloy, Cotter Pin, and Sylvester Simian come charging onto the set. We learn that Galaxy Central has ordered Brock to pilot the Triton *backwards through time to ancient Palestine. The best data suggest that Jerusalem is about to spawn a potentially obnoxious religion, and the Rocket Rangers have come to cancel it. A scowling Jesus, an indignant Peter, and a curious Mary listen as Brock trumpets the virtues of scientific rationality, whereupon the insane Messiah invites everyone to share a meal of bread and wine, explaining that the former will transmogrify into his body and the latter into his blood.*

The instant the Eucharist ends, a diseased and handicapped beggar enters, scissoring forward on crutches and brimming with hope that the renowned faith-healer from Galilee will rehabilitate him. Jesus lays his hands on the blind and crippled leper. Nothing happens. "Miracles are like the gods," Cotter Pin remarks, "capricious, cruel, and wholly unreliable."

While Jesus ponders the failed healing, Sylvester Simian scratches his hairy armpits and outlines "a famous materialist account of human origins, Charles Darwin's theory of evolution by natural selection." Jesus and Peter take exception to this irritating conjecture, and they vent their frustration by breaking apart Lazarus's furniture, improvising cudgels from the wreckage, and menacing the Rocket Rangers. A theological donnybrook follows, with the Galilean and his disciple banging on the impervious torsos of the robot and the gorilla. Suddenly a female voice rises above the brawl. The Demivirgin Mary confesses that, while her heart remains pledged to "the God of my Fathers and the Supreme

Being of my Mothers," she doubts that metaphysical accounts of the universe have a future.

"Tune in next Sunday for another iconoclastic installment of Not By Bread Alone,*" the announcer declares. "Our forthcoming presentation is an original drama by Robert Ingersoll, 'If God Created the Universe, Then Who Created God?' "*

Fade-out. Cut to title card, WHO CREATED GOD? *Dissolve to NBC logo.*

"There," I said, nervously fingering Connie's borrowed motorcycle jacket. "It's finished. What do you think?"

"I think I'm going to throw up," she said.

"This must be hard on you." I brushed her shoulder. "It's hard on me, and I don't even *believe* in God."

Connie squinted at a row of mounted *Catholic Anarchist* front pages, their headlines proclaiming LYNCHINGS ON THE RISE IN JIM CROW MISSISSIPPI and KKK RALLIES IN SAVANNAH and HUNGER IN AMERICA: A NATION'S SHAME. She approached the gallery and adjusted all three frames. For her sake, I hoped Joe McCarthy didn't know about Donna Dain's nickel newspaper, to which hundreds of Communists and fellow travelers doubtless subscribed. "I'll say one thing, Kurt. You have a talent for irreverence."

"So do you."

She winced and closed her eyes. "You should've told the lobsters to travel back two centuries and give their stupid award to David Hume instead."

"I found our collaboration most stimulating."

"Some of what we wrote is clever," said Connie in a tone of qualified assent. "The rest is sophomoric scoffing."

Even as she spoke, my imagination received an unwanted visitation from Pazuzu Jones, Demon of Regret. *Connie's dissatisfaction is well founded,* the intruder insisted. *Your script is insufficient—but sophomoric scoffing is the least of it: you must put these monstrous aliens out of business forever.*

I heaved a sigh and said, "Part of me wants to start over. In fact, my friend, I believe that's precisely what we should do."

"Start over?" said Connie.

"Yes."

"From scratch?"

"My dear, we need a whole new script."

"Are you crazy?" protested Connie. "It's four in the morning, and we haven't even cut the mimeo stencils!"

"Here's the problem," I rasped. "Suppose we fool these maniacs on Sunday—what's to keep them from stumbling into some *other* Judeo-Christian program before they leave? That CBS thing, for instance, *Lamp Unto My Feet*? They'll go berserk all over again and call down their death-ray." I shuffled toward the Silex and started brewing more coffee. "Or maybe next year they'll tune in an inspirational broadcast from elsewhere in the galaxy, and then, *zoom,* they're off to eradicate *those* viewers. The challenge, O Connie Osborne, is more formidable than we thought. We must show the lobsters that their *Weltanschauung*—is that the word you philosophers use?—their *Weltanschauung* is fatally flawed."

"*Weltanschauung Schmeltanschauung!* What you're proposing would take a *week* to write, maybe longer!" Joining me by the Silex, Connie seized my arms and shook me vigorously, an encounter I found erotic, though her intention was to reacquaint me with reality. "I might be my brother's keeper, and my sister's, too, but that ideal doesn't extend to followers of *Lamp Unto My Feet,* much less to every damn believer in the galaxy! That way lies madness!"

She relaxed her grip and backed away. For several minutes no words passed between us. The sounds of percolation filled the basement. I poured two mugs of coffee, let mine cool, took a sip. Paradoxically the caffeine calmed me. Connie was right. To start over would be absurd. The hell with Pazuzu Jones.

"*Weltanschauung Schmeltanschauung!*" I declared, then raised my mug and offered my collaborator a toast. "Confusion to the Qualimosans!"

"Confusion worse confounded!" she proclaimed, lifting her Maxwell House aloft.

We clacked our mugs together, then started hunting for the stencils.

Shortly after dawn we ascended the stairs of 378 Bleecker Street, bound for apartment 4R, Connie carrying a dozen mimeographed scripts while I lugged the steel mass of my Underwood. Lenny had transformed the living room into a movie theater, improvising a projector-stand from the coffee table and a screen from a bedsheet. Navigating by the glow of the tungsten-halogen bulb, I set my typewriter in the far corner.

Eliot had gotten his second wind. Seated on the couch between Wulawand and Volavont, he gave the current Lugosi potboiler his undivided attention, as did Lenny, sprawled across the armchair. Marvin, by contrast, lay asleep on the rug, snoring profusely. The salad bowl contained a few inert brown Quickie-Bang kernels. Popcorn nodes littered the cushions like huge dandruff flakes.

"What's this one called?" asked Connie, speaking above the grinding of the projector and the sharp burble of the dialogue spilling from the auxiliary speaker.

"*The Invisible Ray*," said Lenny. "Shhh. It's almost over."

"Mr. Lugosi is playing Dr. Benet, a deluded astro-chemist who believes that too much knowledge can be as dangerous as too little," said Volavont. "Earlier this evening Dr. Benet and his colleague Dr. Rukh traveled to Africa in search of a meteor that, according to the best astronomical evidence, crashed in the jungle eons ago, bringing with it a new element of unknown powers."

Eliot gestured toward Connie's armful of teleplays. "Looks like you got the job done."

"We're professionals," she said, setting the scripts on the dining table.

"Might I glance at your collaboration?" asked Wulawand. "I read English without difficulty."

"It wouldn't interest you," I said. "An educational program about Canadian paper mills. Dry as dust."

"Dr. Rukh eventually found the extraterrestrial rock," said Volavont, "then learned to harness Radium X for benevolent purposes, giving sight to his blind mother."

"This was a *scientific* cure, of course," said Wulawand, "unlike those miracles the actors were rhapsodizing about in that *Bread Alone* rehearsal."

"Exposure to Radium X caused a wondrous change in Dr. Rukh, giving him an incandescent body and an enlightened mind," said Volavont, gesturing toward the screen: a midshot of Boris Karloff clenching his glowing fists before his equally luminous face. "He proceeded to hunt down and exterminate his incurious colleagues, including Dr. Benet."

Wulawand reached into the salad bowl, scooped up the unpopped kernels, and jammed them in her mouth. "Later today, Mr. Eliot Thornhill will give us what he calls 'the ultimate Manhattan tourist experience,' " the lobster reported. "Did you know that a great work of art sprawls beneath this city, an immense three-dimensional installation that the spectator can enter and explore?"

"I figure that our visit to the IRT will take all morning," said Eliot.

Mentally I applauded my imaginative thespian roommate. Evidently he'd bought us the time we needed for our Chock Full O' Nuts script conference. "Ah, yes, the IRT," I said in a bemused tone. "The New York subway system is the most impressive sculpture on the planet." And unlike many of the pieces one finds at the Metropolitan Museum of Art, I thought, it's entirely secular (with the exception of some Saint Luke's Hospital placards the lobsters would never notice). "I'd love to come with you, but Miss Osborne and I must spend the afternoon writing a script about Norwegian fisheries."

"Quiet!" Lenny demanded. "I want to hear the end of the movie!"

All eyes turned to the screen. To prevent Dr. Rukh from committing another murder, Mother Rukh employed her cane to swat a leather hypodermic case from his grasp, thus shattering his vials of the antidote for Radium X poisoning.

"My son, you have broken the first law of science," said Mother Rukh, a character evidently as sympathetic as our Demivirgin Mary.

"A pox on you, Mother Rukh!" shouted Volavont.

"Yes, you're right," rasped Karloff, exuding smoke and exhibiting other symptoms of internal combustion. "It's better this way. Good-bye, Mother."

The radiant Dr. Rukh charged up the stairway to a balcony door and hurled himself through the glass. Transmuting into a ball of fire, he plummeted to the street below.

"The first law of science," said Connie. "I wonder what she meant by that."

"Never conduct serious research in the Carpathians?" Lenny suggested.

"Refrain from killing sprees?" offered Eliot.

"Refrain from *unnecessary* killing sprees," Volavont corrected him.

"First do no harm?" I proposed.

"Unless the future of reason is at stake," said Wula-wand.

After Lenny finished rewinding *The Invisible Ray*, Eliot began arguing that the Qualimosans' trench coats and slouch hats would not make them sufficiently inconspicuous during the subway tour, and I had to agree. The solution, we soon decided, lay in the talents of our across-the-hall neighbor, an artist named Chet Sargent. Although Eliot had lost his job as a palace guard when *The King and I* ended its run in September, he still boasted one of the healthiest bank balances on Bleecker Street, and he was happy to fund the salvation of two million Christians.

Grateful for the commission, his first in six weeks, Chet took two 24" x 32" slabs of plywood, adorned each with an elegant codfish, then added an advertisement for a nonexistent restaurant: EXPERIENCE FINE DINING AT CAPTAIN CABOT'S SEAFOOD TAVERN—MORNINGSIDE HEIGHTS. A second pair of plywood sheets received an image of a cabin cruiser and a caption touting an alleged service for sportsmen: LONG ISLAND CHARTER BOATS, INC.—CATCH YOUR DINNER IN THE SOUND—RESULTS GUARANTEED. Leather shoulder-straps provided the *coups de grâce,* turning the paintings into sandwich boards.

While Eliot supervised construction of the Qualimosans' disguises, Connie got on the phone to NBC. First she spoke to someone in the art department, directing him to prepare two new title cards, one reading THE MADONNA AND THE STARSHIP, the other asking WHO CREATED GOD? Next she talked to an assistant props manager. Owing to the last-minute addition of a mêlée, she explained, the dining table and the benches on the Lazarus set must be replaced with breakaway furniture.

"You're right, Randy," she said. "Brawls don't normally figure in *Not By Bread Alone,* but it all makes sense in context."

She cradled the handset, and I straightaway called

Saul Silver. Wulawand and Volavont, I explained, were indeed extraterrestrials. Their spaceship was orbiting the Earth, their shuttle lay camouflaged in Rockefeller Center, and my colleague Connie Osborne and I had less than twenty-four hours to produce a teleplay congruent with the invaders' logical-positivist worldview, lest a mass murder occur. We'd arranged to sequester Wulawand and Volavont for the next five hours or so, but would Saul be willing to have them over as dinner guests? Indeed, might he detain them till morning, subsequently tuning in *Not By Bread Alone* and keeping me apprised, via telephone, of their reaction while Connie directed the broadcast?

"You're asking the editor of *Andromeda*," said Saul, "a man who prides himself on his scientific curiosity, if he might conceivably value tête-à-têtes with two intelligent beings from outer space?"

"Silly question."

"What do they eat?"

"Apparently they're omnivores. You got any macaroni and cheese? It needn't be kosher."

"Ha, ha, ha. Yes, I've got macaroni and cheese. How's your edge-of-the-universe novelette coming along?"

"Slowly. I've been preoccupied."

At 11:30 A.M. Connie, Eliot, the lobsters, and I entered West 4th Street Station, my valise bulging with the cloaked Zorningorg Prize, the trinocular goggles, and all twelve copies of the teleplay. Still fetchingly attired in Lenny's motorcycle jacket, Connie approached the newsstand and purchased that morning's *Herald Tribune*.

She immediately wished she hadn't. DYLAN THOMAS DEAD AT THIRTY-EIGHT proclaimed the headline in the lower left corner. PNEUMONIA CLAIMS WELSH BARD IN SAINT VINCENT'S HOSPITAL ran the subhead.

"I hope he raged," said Connie, scanning the article.

"I'm sure he did," I said.

"God rest his soul."

Wulawand and Volavont followed us as we descended to the platform for the uptown A, B, and C trains, both aliens eager to begin the first phase of their cultural adventure, a protracted northward journey to the 207th Street Station near the Harlem River. Doubtless owing to the sandwich boards affixed to their chests and spines like a conquistador's armor, the invertebrates attracted little notice. I told Eliot to meet us on the steps of the American Museum of Natural History at four o'clock, a plan that would presumably allow Connie and me to hand the crustaceans off to Saul and still keep our evening appointment at the White Horse Tavern.

The A train whooshed out of the tunnel and screeched to a halt. Connie and I bid the three IRT tourists farewell, then climbed back to daylight, walked to Prince Street Station, and took the N train to Herald Square.

Our Galilean rabbi, Ezra Heifetz, a swarthy man who

uncannily resembled Warner Sallman's iconic Jesus painting, had already secured a booth at Chock Full O' Nuts. Shortly after sidling into the compartment, Connie and I were joined by the muscular Calder Bolling and the massive Joel Seddok, of Cotter Pin and Sylvester Simian fame respectively. A Negro employee appeared—racial pluralism had been a Chock Full O' Nuts hiring norm even before Jackie Robinson became the company's vice president—and took our orders. We all selected the house specialties: coffee, egg sandwiches, a plateful of brownies. I glanced at my watch. Noon on the dot. Twenty-two hours till show time.

Waiting for our lunch to arrive, the five of us traded autobiographical anecdotes. Until this moment I hadn't realized that Calder had gotten his start as a Venusian gangster in a Republic serial called *Ghouls of the Stratosphere*, nor had I known that, after a knee injury terminated his wrestling career (and exempted him from the Army), Joel had reinvented himself portraying gorillas in horror comedies of the Bowery-Boys-East-Side-Kids-Three-Stooges variety, a résumé that put him in the running for the semicoveted role of Sylvester. As for Ezra, it turned out that incarnating Jesus was something of a family tradition, his grandfather having played the part in D. W. Griffith's *Intolerance*, his great uncle in *Ben-Hur*, and he himself in the recent MGM remake of *Quo Vadis*.

"Here's the funny thing," said Ezra. "We're Jews."

"So was Jesus," noted Connie, distributing three scripts from the stack.

"I can compound the irony," said Ezra. "We're *secular* Jews."

"Jesus was, too, according to Donna Dain," said Connie. "She believes his intention was to end religion and replace it with morality."

The waiter reappeared, orders in hand. As we savored our meals, I offered a full account of the awards ceremony, the crustaceans' scandalized reaction to the "Sitting Shivah" rehearsal, the incinerated dressmaker's dummy, and our efforts to convince Wulawand and Volavont that *Not By Bread Alone* was sacrilegious. By way of countering our three actors' evident skepticism, I removed the Zorningorg Prize from my valise, set the trophy on the table, pulled away the cardigan, and, passing the goggles to Ezra, invited him to peer into the incandescent heart of Qualimosan culture.

The artifact proved persuasive, not only for Ezra but also for Calder and Joel. Something uncanny had fallen into my hands, a hallucination-machine whose provenance was either extraterrestrial or something equally fantastic. The instant I cloaked the prize once again our actors entered into a state of suspended disbelief and set about perusing "The Madonna and the Starship."

"I have trouble believing Ogden's on board with this," said Ezra upon turning the last page. "He's more reverent than God."

"Ogden's taking a vacation," said Connie. "I'll be in the control room on Sunday, calling the shots. I'm counting on you all to show up in character and off the book. Come to conference room C at eight o'clock sharp."

"In other words, we're directing ourselves," said Calder, frowning.

"What other choice is there?" Connie replied.

"We could assassinate the Qualimosans," Calder suggested.

"The X-13 has already been placed on standby alert," I explained. "If the navigator of the aliens' spaceship, a creature called Yaxquid, doesn't hear from Wulawand by twenty minutes after ten tomorrow, the death-ray will fire automatically."

"What if we just lock 'em up somewhere?" asked Joel. "The price of their freedom will be deactivating the X-13."

"Assault Wulawand and Volavont?" said Connie. "They probably have sidearm blasters. Don't you ever watch *Brock Barton and His Rocket Rangers*?"

"Believe me, our best hope is this script," I said, "not some reckless Errol Flynn derring-do."

"Since the death-ray will be riding the NBC carrier wave, maybe we could simply disconnect the transmitter before the broadcast," Joel persisted. "Okay, sure, hundreds of thousands of *Bread Alone* viewers would probably change channels to some *other* religious program, for which the network will never forgive us, but that's better than letting everybody die."

"I don't mind boosting the ratings for *Lamp Unto My Feet*," said Connie, "but the Qualimosans *themselves* might switch to that show, and then the jig would *really* be up."

Calder tapped his script with a silver-plated cigarette lighter. "You know what's going to happen, don't you? After this thing hits the airwaves, we'll all be out of work."

"Worse than that," said Joel. "Everybody connected with *Bread Alone* and *Brock Barton* will be out of work."

"Speaking for myself, I'm looking on the bright side." Ezra dunked a brownie in his coffee. He bit off a soggy morsel, chewed pensively, and laid a palm on his script. "A Messiah driven mad by his premature burial," he said in measured tones. "Hey, Connie, hey, Kurt—this is meaty stuff. Jesus as Quixote, as Lear, Ahab, Raskolnikov. I'm salivating like Pavlov's dog. Sure, I'll probably get some bad press in *Daily Variety*, 'Yid Thespian Ridicules Redeemer in Blasphemous Broadcast,' but, hey, I can live with it."

"Actually, I'm pretty darned excited, too," said Joel. "How often does an actor get to play a gorilla who introduces Jesus Christ to Charles Darwin?"

"Thanks for the line, 'Miracles are like the gods—capricious, cruel, and wholly unreliable,'" said Calder. "Delicious."

"I see just one hitch," said Ezra. "So the Qualimosans go home without committing mass murder—great—but how do we know they won't monitor a regular *Bread Alone* broadcast next month and realize they've been hornswoggled?"

"Kurt worries about that, too," said Connie. "In theory we could write and produce a very different script, calculated to make the crustaceans see the limitations of their *Weltanschauung*, but the clock is against us."

"Let's not allow the perfect to become the enemy of the good," Calder told the group.

"Saving two million lives sounds like a fine morning's work to me," added Joel. "I think we should settle for that."

Ezra snorted and said nothing.

I unveiled my trophy, slipped on the visor, and surveyed the nearest facet. No doubt my sleep-deprived brain was playing tricks on me, but I thought I saw an impish creature cavorting across a meadow strewn with glittering diamonds. *Calder is right,* the Demon of Regret told me, *you must not let the perfect become the enemy of the good—but neither should you let the good become the friend of the atrocious.*

"By the way, this lunch is on NBC," said Connie, signaling our waiter. "I have a subsistence expense account."

"Then let's have another cup of coffee," said Joel.

"More brownies," said Calder.

"The best bottle of champagne in the Chock Full O' Nuts cellar," said Ezra.

I continued to contemplate the iridescent triangle. The Demon of Regret vanished. Like an immense colony of fireflies, the diamonds rose from the meadow to ornament a seamless black sky, forming constellations that presumably illustrated some Qualimosan equivalent of pagan mythology. But the substance of these stories was opaque to me, narratives from another world, so I closed my eyes, removed the goggles, and, like a magician covering a bird cage prior to making a canary disappear, dropped the cardigan back over my prize.

4.
ANYTHING FOR OVALTINE

The instant I beheld Eliot and the Qualimosans milling around on the steps of the American Museum of Natural History, the aliens still bedecked in their sandwich boards, I concluded that my roommate's scheme had succeeded. Waving their subway maps around like pennants, the lobsters comported themselves with the glee of children who'd just seen an especially splendid performance by the Rockettes. Of course, it would be foolish to take Wulawand and Volavont themselves to see the famous Radio City Music Hall show—they were certain to become bored and flee into the metropolis at large, soon spotting evidence that Earthlings were more enamored of the metaphysical than they'd assumed—but luckily I had an ace named Saul Silver up my sleeve.

"Nowhere on Qualimosa can an aficionado of the arts visit anything as magnificent as your Interborough Rapid Transit," Wulawand declared.

"Sorry we couldn't join you," I said, setting down my valise, its interior crammed with my award and the nine remaining teleplays. "At least Miss Osborne and I finished our script about Norwegian fisheries."

"O Eliot Thornhill, you are a virtuoso tour guide," said Volavont to my roommate.

"Not the first time an unemployed actor has worked as a docent," said Eliot.

"We especially enjoyed the subterranean gallery called Times Square," said Volavont.

" 'Come and meet those dancing feet,' " sang Connie, " 'on the avenue I'm takin' you to, Forty-Second Street.' "

"Mr. Thornhill performed that same song for us," said Volavont. " ' Little nifties from the Fifties, innocent and sweet,' " he sang. " 'Sexy ladies from the Eighties, who are indiscreet.' " A carillon of *squonk, squonk, squonk* laughter pealed from his throat. " 'They're side by side, they're glorified, where the underworld can meet the elite, naughty, bawdy, gaudy, sporty Forty-Second Street'! "

"Speaking of the Eighties, our next destination is just around the corner," I said. "Saul Silver, editor of America's premier science-fiction magazine, has invited you to dine with him on macaroni and cheese. Reading *Andromeda* as a teenager made me the atheist rationalist logical positivist I am today."

"We shall happily accede to Mr. Silver's request," said Wulawand. "On Qualimosa we, too, have science-fiction periodicals, although *Rocket Sagas* and *Comet Angst* are surely inferior to your *Andromeda*."

"Will you and Miss Osborne be joining the party?" asked Volavont.

"I'm afraid we've got an emergency conference at the studio," I replied, shaking my head. "You'll find Mr. Silver a little peculiar—he suffers from agoraphobia—but he's got the finest mind in the business."

Eliot announced that he must now "revisit the aesthetic pleasures of the IRT," as he had a ticket to see Arthur Kennedy and E. G. Marshall in *The Crucible* that night at the Martin Beck and wanted "to grab some dinner first at a midtown automat." Before Eliot strode away, the lobsters offered him their gratitude for "a visually munificent and acoustically nutritive afternoon."

I decided to accompany my roommate on his one-block walk to the 81st Street Station, taking the opportunity to thank him for confining Wulawand and Volavont to a secular zone during the Chock Full O' Nuts meeting.

"So how's the big broadcast shaping up?" he asked.

"I'm guardedly optimistic. That said, if you know anybody who watches *Not By Bread Alone*, tell him to skip tomorrow's installment."

Ten minutes later, Connie, the crustaceans, and I stood shoulder-to-carapace in the atrium of Saul Silver's building. I pressed the buzzer. Gladys trundled up from the basement, admitted us to the foyer, and promptly lost her composure, chortling like a schoolgirl being mischievous in church.

"You Flash Gordon guys will do *anything* to get into Mr. Silver's magazine, won't you?" she said, looking Wulawand in her compound eye. "He'll love your getups, but if you *really* want to impress him, bring him a blow-up floozy next time." She offered me a conspiratorial wink. "He thinks I don't know about Zelda and Zoey."

"We are not Flash Gordon guys," Wulawand insisted, "and we have no desire to write for *Andromeda*."

"Mr. Silver is expecting us," added Volavont. "We are here to eat macaroni and talk about the cosmos."

"Who are Zelda and Zoey?" Connie asked me as Gladys guided us up the stairs.

"Sexy ladies from the Eighties," I said.

Arriving at the threshold of apartment 3C, the adjacent landing still crowded with back issues of *Amazing*, *Astounding*, and *Fantastic*, Gladys disengaged the lock and ushered us into the living room. Saul's fox terrier leaped off the couch and began barking at the lobsters, calming down the instant Gladys said, "Now, Ira, that's no way to greet folks who've come all the way from Neptune to see us."

Saul was seated behind his desk, scribbling furiously in the margins of a manuscript, his face obscured by three precarious piles of unsolicited fiction, most of it residing in sealed Manila envelopes. The Admiral TV was tuned to a Dodgers game—which made no sense, the season having ended two months earlier.

"Forgive me for not rising," said Saul to the lobsters. "I have a condition."

"You need never ask our forgiveness, O Saul Silver, whose magazine made Kurt Jastrow the atheist rationalist logical positivist he is today," said the female crustacean, removing her sandwich board. "Call me Wulawand."

"I am Volavont." The male crustacean likewise shed his disguise, then employed his triadic orbs to scan the exhibit of *Andromeda* cover paintings.

"Ebbets Field?" I said, pointing to the TV. "What the hell are the Dodgers doing playing in November?"

"That's a documentary movie about Jackie Robinson," Saul explained. "A real *mensch*. When he gets too old to play the game, I hope they retire his number." He scrutinized the lobsters. "I saw you on my cathode-ray tube yesterday, giving Kurt his award. For three years now, Uncle Wonder has been saving the galaxy from God, and it was high time the galaxy stopped taking him for granted. Uncle Wonder, I mean, not God."

"Maybe your magazine will receive a Zorningorg Prize some day," said Wulawand.

"That would certainly ramp up the circulation." Saul pitched me a grin. "Is that your trophy in the bag, Kurt? Bring it here."

I set my valise on Saul's desk and removed the cloaked prism. "It's like Medusa," I said, retrieving the trinocular goggles. "Perseus had his shield, and you'll need this visor."

Instead of donning the goggles and contemplating the kaleidoscopic triangles, Saul pointed to my colleague and said, "And this darling creature must be Connie Osborne. *Enchanté.*"

"*Moi aussi,*" said Connie.

With all the nonchalance I could muster, I slipped a copy of "The Madonna and the Starship" from my valise and surreptitiously inserted it in a slush pile. "Connie equates *Andromeda* with something she calls 'that Buck Rogers stuff,' but we're friends anyway."

"Permit me to suggest that even Buck Rogers stuff is not Buck Rogers stuff," said Saul to Connie.

"I intend to look into your famous publication," she said. "Where should I start? I've heard almost anything by Kurt Jastrow is worth reading."

"A gift for Miss Osborne," said Saul, lifting an *Andromeda* from his desk and passing it to me. I delivered the issue to Connie. "Our latest number, hot off the presses," the great man continued. "Are you favorably disposed toward satire, my dear? Then I recommend 'A Child of the Millennium' by Manfred Glass. If you're a ban-the-bomb sort of gal, try 'The Last Countdown' by Terrence Murgeon. As it happens, they're both coming over later for our Saturday night poker game. Their insomnia's even worse than mine."

I'd participated in a West 82nd Street seven-card stud

tournament only once in my life, and that was quite enough. The pulp-meisters of Prospect Park—Manny Glass and Terry Murgeon—had emptied my pockets to the last speck of lint.

"I love poker," said Connie. "Alas, Kurt and I'll be working at the studio during your bluffing marathon."

"I love it, too," said Wulawand.

"You have poker on Qualimosa?" asked Saul.

"The rules are so logical and self-evident that the game has evolved independently on many worlds, as did chess and mahjong," said Volavont. "Seven-card stud, I daresay, is a universal constant, rather like electron mass and the speed of light."

"Then we'll have to deal you both in tonight," said Saul. "We'll play till mid-morning, then flip on the TV and look at that amusing religious satire—what's it called?—*Not By Bread Alone*."

"As Mr. Jastrow and Miss Osborne will tell you, we have taken a profound interest in tomorrow's installment," said Wulawand, retrieving both the ocarina-shaped transceiver and the gold lamé cloth from beneath her carapace. "Shortly after the program begins, we may have to suspend this impervious veil in front of the picture tube, contact the navigator of our orbiting spaceship"—she stroked the sinister sweet potato—"and speak with him concerning an X-13 death-ray."

"Our goal being to exterminate a hive of irrationalist vermin thriving on your planet," said Volavont.

"Irrationalist vermin deserve nothing better," said Saul, assuming an impeccable poker face.

"Perhaps you can settle a controversy for us," said Volavont. "In a high-low game, the best possible low hand is ace-two-three-four-five, correct?"

"Uh-huh," said Saul.

"But would that sequence not constitute a straight?" asked Wulawand.

"Not according to the standard rules."

"I told you so," said Volavont, *squonk-squonk-squonking* in Wulawand's face.

"I'm hoping that, before Manny and Terry get here, you marvelous invertebrates might help me catch up on my work." Saul rested his hand on the tallest tower of submissions. "You'll be able to tell within a page or two whether a manuscript's worth reading."

"On Qualimosa the science-fiction authors are stuck in a rut," said Wulawand. "Last month *Rocket Sagas* and *Comet Angst* both published stories that end, 'And her name was Eve.' "

"You have an Adam and Eve legend on your planet?" asked Saul.

"You would be surprised how many Milky Way bards sing of a primordial sexually-reproducing couple," said Volavont. "On Qualimosa we call them Filbone and Fonia. The irrationalist faction in our civil war regards them as historical figures."

"Another breakthrough for Alpha Enterprises!" I

declared. " 'Subscribe to *Andromeda*, the only science-fiction magazine whose slush pile is read by actual aliens!' "

"I wonder, would the average SF writer rather have his story accepted by me or a couple of guest editors from Procyon?" Saul slipped on the goggles, pulled away the cardigan, and leaned toward the prism. "Good heavens!"

"Your question is not difficult," said Wulawand. "He would rather his story were blessed by *you*, O Saul Silver."

"If I believed in a Supreme Being, I would swear I'm staring into his brain!" Saul declared. "A billion divine neurons, flashing on and off! Apocalyptic glowworms! The electric eels of *Ein Sof*!" Panting and gulping, he removed the goggles and set them on his desk. "There is no God, and he lives in this prism."

"Are you all right, Mr. Silver?" Gladys inquired.

"Perseus was lucky he didn't have agoraphobia," said Saul, nodding. "Even a diluted Medusa is too much for me."

Returning to the great man's desk, I cloaked the trophy with the cardigan. "There's a teleplay of interest in this pile," I whispered, setting my palm on the relevant stack of manuscripts. "Read it if you get a chance. Don't pass it to the lobsters by mistake."

I packed away the Zorningorg Prize and ferried the valise across the room. Cupping my free hand beneath Connie's arm, I guided her toward the door.

"We'll try to return in time for the broadcast," I told

Saul and his guests as I escorted my colleague out of the apartment. "Otherwise, enjoy the show!"

"Praised be the gods of logic!" exclaimed Wulawand.

"All hail the avatars of doubt!" declared Volavont.

"*Vita brevis, ars longa!*" shouted Saul.

As dusk seeped into the pocks and pores of Greenwich Village, Connie and I trudged down Hudson Street, morosely preparing one another for the worst. Three of the five remaining actors we hoped to recruit were *Not By Bread Alone* regulars, and while Connie didn't know them well, she suspected that our presumed apostle Peter, our intended leper, and our hypothetical Demivirgin Mary felt rather more protective toward Western civilization's favorite religion than did our secular Jewish Jesus. Once they learned just how far "The Madonna and the Starship" went in sneering at the sacred, they might change their minds and bow out.

Transfixed by foreboding, we entered the White Horse Tavern and strode past the crowded bar to a cramped dining space featuring dark oak walls, Dashiell Hammett shadows, and a pale plaster horse the size of a lamb. We proceeded to the back room. Two Rocket Rangers and a disciple of Jesus awaited us, seated in an alcove beneath a frieze of pseudo-Tiffany stained glass, both *Brock Barton* actors nursing golden beers.

Approaching the gloomy niche, Connie suddenly

groaned. She slouched against the wall and sucked in a deep breath.

"On Wednesday night," she explained to the troupe, "in this very alcove, I saw Dylan Thomas consume what would prove to be his last shot of alcohol."

"Shall we move to another table?" asked Hollis Wright, the reasonably handsome and adequately talented actor who portrayed Brock Barton.

"No, but we should down a round of whiskies tonight in Mr. Thomas's honor," said Connie, installing herself at the head of the table.

"I don't drink," said Clement Sayles, our presumed Peter, a tall ectomorph with a diffident beard he'd probably grown for his *Bread Alone* appearance.

"I'll be your proxy," said the stumpy and hyperkinetic Jimmy Breeze, better known as Ducky Malloy. "I confess to a fondness for whiskey."

" 'And death shall have no dominion,' " said Wilma Lamont, gliding toward the alcove. The actress we'd marked for Mary was an earthy woman whose wry eyes and mischievous lips betrayed a certain lewdness of temperament—not anyone's default image of the Blessed Virgin, but Ogden Lynx was famous for casting against type. "He was a great writer. Evidently I've got a crack at playing Rosie Probert when the Poetry Center revives *Under Milk Wood* next year. They just signed Hugh Griffith for Captain Cat."

Now our intended leper, the wan and cadaverous

Gully Lomax, joined the gathering. "Is Ogden coming?" he asked.

"This isn't an Ogden sort of project," said Connie, distributing the scripts. "Last night Kurt gave you a rough idea why we can't broadcast my original teleplay, and now he'll fill in the details."

"First let's get some food on the table," I said.

We placed our orders, including the local liquid delicacy, a mixture of porter and ale, then indulged in autobiographical revelations, a conversation keyed to Gully's fear that, owing to a dalliance with the Young Communist League, "Joe McCarthy's bloodhounds have caught my scent."

Within fifteen minutes the various cheeseburgers, Reuben sandwiches, soft drinks, and beers arrived. As the meal progressed, I told the actors everything I knew about the Qualimosan crisis. Anticipating their objections to our baroque solution, I explained that waylaying the lobsters was not a possibility, since the X-13 death-ray would strike automatically at 10:20 A.M. I concluded by remarking that "an orbiting Sword of Damocles" hung over the heads of two million innocent TV viewers, "but I feel confident we can sheath the blade."

I set the Zorningorg Prize on the table, then removed the cardigan and delivered the trinocular goggles to Clement, who promptly descended to the prism's hallucinatory core. Emerging, he passed the trophy to Wilma—and so it went, actor after actor, until the entire troupe had entered into a condition of primordial wonderment.

"We've got to work this pyramid thing into a *Brock Barton* episode," said Hollis, stroking the prize.

"Another day's discussion." I cloaked the artifact and returned it to my valise.

Taking up their scripts, our cast read "The Madonna and the Starship" with more sympathy than any pointedly satiric if occasionally sophomoric teleplay had ever received in human history.

"Given the time crunch, I can't offer you much directorial guidance," said Connie after everyone had scanned the final page. "Each of you must plumb his soul for plausible motivations. May I assume you're all willing to play the game?"

"You can count on Brock Barton," said Hollis.

"And the apostle Peter," said Clement, lighting a Pall Mall.

"Maybe this whole thing will turn out to be a hoax," said Wilma, "like what Orson Welles did on the radio with those Martians, but we still gotta see it through."

"This is a great opportunity for me," said Gully evenly. "I'm always looking to fatten my McCarthy dossier."

"It's just crazy enough to work," declared Jimmy, another line I'd promised myself I would never use in a *Brock Barton* episode. "That said, I'm telling my sister and her husband to watch *Lamp Unto My Feet* instead."

Connie issued the essential imperatives—conference

room C, 8:00 A.M., lines down pat—then added, "God willing, we'll send these dreadful aliens home before they can hurt anybody."

"Great, but there's just one problem," said Hollis, flicking a bit of corned beef off his script. "Three years ago I was about to autograph my Brock Barton contract when Mr. Spalding pointed out a clause that Kellogg's had inserted at the last minute. The whole matter seemed trivial at the time, so I went ahead and signed."

Jimmy took a large swallow of black and tan. "And the clause said—?"

"That I can't portray Brock Barton under any circumstances—including guest stints on other shows and live appearances at supermarket openings and such—without making a pitch for Sugar Corn Pops twice each hour."

"We don't need this, Hollis," I said. "We really don't."

"Turns out that Ovaltine added the same sort of clause," he elaborated.

"You're spoiling my appetite," I muttered.

"Here's an idea," said Connie. "Ten minutes into the new script, Jesus has everybody sit down to a Eucharist meal, right?"

"Shazam!" cried an excited Wilma. " 'Eat these measures of Sugar Corn Pops, for they are my body. Drink this Ovaltine, for it is my blood.' "

"At which juncture Brock steps in and pitches both products, like he's done a thousand times before!" exclaimed Hollis.

"Okay, that should work," I said, scanning our troupe. "I assume the rest of you have no such catches in your contracts."

"No catches, but I think we could do a lot more with my blind and crippled leper," said Gully. "He's our Job figure—right?—the blameless victim who's not afraid to put God in the dock. So how about giving me a knockout dungheap filibuster? Jehovah is a monster, a sadist, a cosmic vivisectionist who takes pleasure in his creatures' suffering."

"I see your point, but we've got to keep the show down to twenty-five minutes," said Connie. "If we encroach on *Corporal Rex, Wonder Dog of the NYPD*, there'll be hell to pay. But assuming things go at a fast enough clip, I'll have the floor manager give you the high sign, and you can deliver a succinct Jobian rant."

"Too bad you had to drop Mary's other sons," said Wilma. "Your aliens would love to see my virginity take it on the chin. Maybe I could tell Jesus, 'As a little boy, you were quite a handful, especially compared to your brothers.'"

"I like that," said Connie. "Scratch your speech about the preschool Jesus kicking the puppy and add what you just said."

I took a final swallow of black and tan. "And then Ezra replies, 'Well, naturally I was a handful. I'm God, you know.'"

"Great!" exclaimed Connie.

"As long as we're writing our own material," said Clement, puffing on his Pall Mall, "let's have Peter make an Oscar Wilde sort of overture to Jesus, who hugs his disciple passionately and says, 'On this church I will get my rocks off.'"

"No!" cried Gully, slamming his palm on the table.

"Are you insane?" Wilma asked Clement.

"Just a suggestion."

"It's time we ordered the final round," said Connie, gesturing the waitress into our vicinity. "Please bring us seven watered-down whiskies," she told the bored young woman, "two bowls of pretzels, and a maudlin anecdote about the late Dylan Thomas."

Eager to learn their lines and disappear into their revised personae, the five players exited the White Horse Tavern at seven o'clock. Connie and I lingered, drinking coffee and convincing each other that the changes we'd just endorsed were for the better. Shortly after seven-thirty I called Ezra on the tavern's payphone, explained the Kellogg's contract crisis, and gave him his new lines for the Eucharist scene plus his riposte to Mary's declaration that he'd been a difficult child.

"This is juicy stuff, full of subtext," he enthused. "*Bread Alone* will go out with a bang, won't it?"

"The biggest," I said. "Bring all the necessary breakfast cereal props, okay?"

"Sure."

"Ovaltine, too."

"You got it."

Next I rang up Saul, who told me Manny and Terry had arrived at 59 West 82nd Street a half-hour ago. Everybody was getting along like gangbusters. Already Saul, the *Andromeda* writers, and the lobsters had played two hands of seven-card stud, Manny taking the first pot with a flush, Volavont winning the second with three jacks.

"Before the game, Wulawand found an extraordinary first-contact story in the pile," said Saul. Lowering his voice, he added, "I like the script, Kurt. *Mazel tov.*"

"It keeps getting better."

"Too bad it leaves the aliens' *Weltanschauung* intact."

"We mustn't let the perfect become the enemy of the good."

"True enough, but I'm going to have Manny and Terry read it on the sly. If we get any bright ideas, I'll call you first thing in the morning."

As the watered-down whiskies evaporated from our brains, Connie and I left the White Horse and ambled toward Father Demo Square, looking for a taxi.

"Did Clement really say, 'On this church I will get my rocks off'?" she asked.

"I think it was the beer talking," I said, my gaze alighting on Our Lady of Pompeii School, its neo-Renaissance façade commanding the corner of Bleecker Street and Leroy.

"He wasn't drinking," Connie noted.

Pompeii. The supreme seismic disaster of the First Century A.D. Squalls of fiery ash descending from on high, promiscuously incinerating multitudes. If Our Lady was helpless to prevent Vesuvius from carbonizing a Roman city, what made me think I could defeat the Qualimosans?

"Connie, I can't do it," I moaned. Setting down my valise, I embraced a NO PARKING sign.

"Do what?"

"I can't *think* on that scale. Nobody can. Two million innocent viewers. The human mind wasn't *built* for such statistics."

"I thought you were a science-fiction writer. You deal routinely in nuclear holocausts and Martians wiping out Manhattan."

"That's all fantasy," I said. "It's all Buck Rogers stuff."

"Don't you remember what Mr. Silver told me today? Even Buck Rogers stuff is not Buck Rogers stuff."

Connie's words proved peculiarly comforting. I broke free of the No Parking sign and stood erect. Buck Rogers was fantasy, and I couldn't answer for Our Lady, but good old Saul was real, and so was Uncle Wyatt, chief priest of the church of cosmic astonishment. The show must go on.

"Taxi!" Connie shouted.

———

Naturally I assumed Connie would instruct the Yellow Cab driver to take us to our respective apartments, so we might try for a full night's sleep before raising the curtain on our teleplay. Instead she specified Rockefeller Center. "After this evening's broadcast of *The Original Amateur Hour*," she explained, squeezing my hand, "we can appropriate Studio Two at nine o'clock, aim the cameras at the *Bread Alone* set, and do a slapdash tech rehearsal."

"Isn't Sid Caesar in Studio Two at nine?" I asked, dandling the Zorningorg Prize on my knee.

"Nope, One—and then comes *Your Hit Parade* in Three," said Connie. "This will be fun, Kurt. You'll get to play all the parts, and I'll get to pretend I'm Ida Lupino."

By the time we'd gone through a security check and made our way to Studio Two, *The Original Amateur Hour* had wrapped: lights off, control room dark, cameras inert. We hurried to the *Bread Alone* set. As conceived by the network's art director, Lazarus's dining room boasted an elegant simplicity: white stucco walls, brown amphorae, potted palm tree, wooden table holding a bowl filled with plastic grapes and wax figs, picture window opening onto Jesus's tomb. A somber young man in a goatee and black turtleneck darted about, gripping a six-pigment palette and touching up the décor. He paused in his labors long enough to introduce himself as Marshall Crompton, then added,

"I don't dig workin' for such a square show, but I gotta buy groceries."

"You're an atheist?" I suggested.

"More of an agnostic anarchist gadfly," Marshall explained. "My path in life was blazed by Pablo Picasso, Allen Ginsberg, and Ernie Kovacs."

"You'll enjoy tonight's tech rehearsal," I said. "We're preparing for our annual tribute to blasphemy."

"Blasphemy?"

"Think Saturnalia. Once a year on this show, we worship the Lord of Misrule."

"Smooth."

Come Sunday morning, of course, Connie would compose each image by relaying orders to the cameramen through their headsets, but for now she and I had to wheel the rigs around ourselves, positioning camera one to deliver a longshot of the set, camera two to cover Jesus's tomb, and three to focus on Mary seated at the table. After passing me a script and stationing the boom mike above the fruit bowl, Connie retreated to the control room, where she fired up the console, drenched the set in klieg illumination, and cued me over the public-address system. Teleplay in hand, I launched into the opening speeches, taking the parts of both Mary and Peter. Marshall seemed amused by the dialogue, especially the apostle explaining how he and his confrère had rescued Jesus with an opiate, and when the time came for the stone to roll away from the tomb, he was happy to show me which off-stage lever to push.

"Here's an idea," I told Marshall. "For the rest of the tech rehearsal, let's have you be Jesus."

"Crazy, man," he replied, then proceeded to enact the teleplay's first big visual moment: the buried-alive Galilean rabbi escaping his crypt.

"A word of friendly advice," I said. "Don't watch the broadcast tomorrow."

"But I'm diggin' it," said Marshall.

"We have reason to believe the navigator of an orbiting alien spaceship intends to retrofit a death-ray onto the *Bread Alone* carrier wave."

"Cool."

For the next three hours, Marshall and I ran through the script (variously incarnating the perplexed Mary, the conniving Peter, the mad Jesus, the bitter leper, the chivalrous Brock, the facetious Ducky, the unflappable robot, and the philosophical gorilla), while Connie stayed in the control room and jotted down ideas for lighting effects, dolly moves, and camera angles. Bringing "The Madonna and the Starship" to its jeopardized audience would be less like directing a teleplay than covering a Dodgers game or the Macy's Thanksgiving Day Parade, but I sensed that Connie was unwilling to settle for tedious longshots and bland midshots. When a given moment called for a close-up, she would by-God deliver the goods.

The rehearsal ended shortly after 11:00 P.M. I bid Marshall good night, gave him ten bucks for his troubles, and, taking hold of my valise, climbed the stairs to Connie's sanctum. I entered quietly, knowing she might be in the midst of a creative meditation, but instead I found her talking on the phone.

With a wary eye I surveyed the console, a science-fictional installation comprising the switching device, the audio mixing board, and a bank of small monitors labeled CAMERA 1, CAMERA 2, CAMERA 3, PREVIEW, AIR, and FILM CHAIN. Everything seemed fully functional. Connie cradled the handset. Having discarded Lenny's motorcycle jacket, which now hung over the back of the technical director's chair, she presented herself to me in the same maroon silk blouse she'd been wearing since we left the studio on Friday afternoon.

"I just told Donna Dain that under no circumstances should anyone at the Saint Francis House watch tomorrow's *Bread Alone* broadcast," she explained.

"I'm too tired to know if I had fun tonight or not," I said. "Was it fun for you?"

A rapturous expression lit Connie's face, and for an instant she radiated the same caliber of sensuality as our Demivirgin Mary. "This is going to work, Kurt! Our masquerade will save the world—I can *feel* it!" She gestured toward my trophy. "Hey, friend, don't you think it's high time I got a good look at that thing?"

I opened my valise, removed the award, and yanked

away the cardigan. Connie donned the goggles, then contemplated the nearest facet, breathing deeply as the artifact romanced her gray matter. She reported seeing a lambent river swirling around a crystalline palace, a fire-breathing gryphon wheeling above an active volcano, and a fountain spouting "the primordial juices of multicellular life."

"And now we can go home and sleep," I said, cloaking the trophy.

"Vita brevis, ars longa!" Connie pulled off the goggles and tapped me on the shoulder. "Home? I have a better idea. Instead of rushing back to Rockefeller Center at the crack of dawn, let's spend the night here. On Thursday they did *The Fourposter* on *Producers Showcase*. The bed's still in Studio Three, and I'm sure we can scare up a cot for you. Ogden keeps an alarm clock in his office."

"I'll sleep better in my own bed."

"What I meant, Kurt Jastrow, is that I have a *really* better idea." She crossed to the technical director's chair, reached inside Lenny's jacket, and removed a cardboard container no larger than a cigarette pack. "Look what your roommate left in his pocket. At first I thought it was his Chesterfields."

I stared at the box in question, with its famous logo of a plumed Trojan helmet against a red background. My pulse performed a paradiddle. "I taught him how to buy those things," I said, inanely.

"Then you must be familiar with their application."

"I suppose so," I croaked—though not as familiar as I might have wished, my experience with rubbers being limited to the actress who'd played the villainous lady botanist in "She Demons of Io," plus a nymphomaniac who worked as a receptionist at *Planet Stories* and twice lured me to the office after hours for a roll in the slush.

"I am likewise prophylactically literate. At Barnard I fell head over heels for a Columbia grad student who understood Spinoza." Connie slipped on the visor once more. "Look at this! It's better than an *Andromeda* cover!"

She passed me the goggles, and I put them on in time to behold a pasture vibrating with iridescent dragonflies and carpeted with coruscating crimson poppies.

" 'O, rest ye, brother mariners, we will not wander more,' " I said, quoting Tennyson's *The Lotos-Eaters* but thinking of Connie's secondary sex characteristics.

" 'They're side by side, they're glorified, where the underworld can meet the elite'!" she sang. "Take me to the fourposter, Kurt. Stay me with flagons. Comfort me with apples. Buck Roger me."

Mesmerized by alien dragonflies, extraterrestrial poppies, and the primordial juices of multicellular life, to say nothing of the imminent masquerade, I careened into Studio Three, Connie at my side, my valise weighed down with my award plus Ogden's alarm clock and the four remaining scripts. Zipped back into Lenny's motorcycle jacket, still muttering song lyrics, Connie headed for the curtain. She pulled it away to reveal the promised bed. *Your Hit Parade* had wrapped a half-hour earlier. The airwaves belonged to local stations. We had the place to ourselves.

"What will your analyst say about this?" I asked.

" 'Naughty, bawdy, gaudy, sporty Forty-Second Street,' " Connie sang.

Until that night my favorite twentieth-century drama had been *Death of a Salesman*, but now it was *The Fourposter* by Jan de Hartog. We scrambled aboard the mattress. The zippers of Connie's jacket parted melodiously. The buttons of her maroon blouse yielded to my trembling fingers. Briefly her bra-clasps challenged my dexterity, but at last the silken chrysalises dropped away.

" 'Though wise men at their end know dark is right,' " Connie recited, undressing me in turn, " 'because their words had forked no lightning, they do not go gentle into that good night.' "

"Tomorrow we fork the lightning!" I exclaimed, though I had no idea what it meant to treat an electrical discharge in that fashion. (If I tried it on *Uncle Wonder's Attic*, I would probably burn down Rockefeller Center.) "Tomorrow we cleave the sun!"

The woman with no use for pulp fiction had a pulp fiction sort of body, *Amazing Stories* hips, *Astounding* thighs, *Fantastic* breasts. My appreciation manifested itself as a boner that could sink an eight ball. Inhaling the sharp medicinal scent, I sheathed my lust in latex. Would I live to see the day when these sublime commodities were advertised on TV? Buy Trojan condoms, with the lubrication already on 'em?

Not surprisingly, I came in less time than it took Buffalo Bob to do a Colgate commercial. Connie proved understanding. Things went better the second time around. Although for us the phenomenon of simultaneous orgasm belonged to some distant *Brock Barton* future, we managed to serve that ideal through successive approximations, whereupon, satiated at last, we fumbled for Ogden's alarm clock.

Connie found it first. She wound it up, setting the bell for seven-thirty. We interlaced our limbs and closed our eyes. Man did not live by bread alone, and neither did woman, but at that moment it seemed as if we might sustain ourselves forever on eros.

But sleep, that fickle physician, refused to visit my side of the bed. Dr. Hypnos paid no house calls to Studio Three. Like a machine shorn of its flywheel, my mind raced uncontrollably. Evidently I'd entered a zone beyond exhaustion, a realm where weariness stimulates a person's brain even as it numbs his flesh.

Monday would mark the beginning of the Brock Barton adventure called "The Space Pirates of Callisto," each chapter followed by an *Uncle Wonder's Attic* install-ment for which I was reasonably well prepared. The subsequent week would bring "The Phantom Asteroid," the teleplay I'd workshopped on Tuesday morning with the Underwood Milkers. I remained fond of the basic conceit: Prince Nihil, the last Nonextant, imprisoning the *Triton*'s crew inside the nightmares of his ethereal ancestors. Nihil. Nihilism. Nothingness. The jejune glamour of the void. The adolescent allure of the abyss.

And suddenly I understood how we might give our visiting invertebrates some ethical backbone.

I rolled over, kissed Connie awake, and cried, "I've got it!"

"Jesus, Kurt, I just fell asleep."

"I see what has to happen in the second half-hour!"

"What has to happen is *Corporal Rex*," said Connie dryly.

"No, that whole series is on celluloid," I noted. "Tomorrow morning we'll tamper with the film chain. They'll repair it later in the week and run the preempted episode *next* Sunday."

"*Corporal Rex* is a *sponsored* show," Connie protested. "Ralston Purina will not go gentle into that good night."

"I don't want to talk about dog food. I want to talk about philosophy." Climbing off the fourposter, I retrieved my boxer shorts. "Remember my script about the Nonextants? You're the expert, but it seems to me our crustaceans aren't really logical positivists at all.

Nor are they atheists, Darwinists, doubters, rationalists, skeptics, sages, or atomists. They're simply—"

"Good God, you're right," said Connie. "They're nihilists."

"It's all clear to me now!" I babbled, strapping on my wristwatch. 2:00 A.M. "Our script is missing two crucial characters. When Saul and his guests tune in 'The Madonna and the Starship' today, Wulawand and Volavont must see *themselves* on the screen. That is, they must see, er, let me think—"

"They must see Zontac and Korkhan, the raygun-toting nihilists from Planet Voidovia!" exclaimed Connie. "The invertebrates who've replaced God with their own megalomania!"

"Perfect!"

"The present draft pits metaphysics against material-ism." Connie slid off the fourposter and started getting dressed. "But unless you're an ancient Greek, dialectic is not enough. The rewrite must turn on—"

"Trialectic?"

"Good!" She raised her hand, made a fist, extended the index finger. "Worldview number one: the Judeans—Mary, Jesus, Peter, and the leper, connoisseurs of the supernatural." Her middle finger emerged. "Worldview number two: our Voidovians—Zontac and Korkhan, acolytes of the abyss." Her ring finger appeared. "And hovering above these incompatible persuasions, worldview number three: the scientific humanists of the space schooner *Triton*—Brock, Ducky, Cotter Pin, and Sylvester, at odds with both the numinous and the nihilistic."

"I knew that Buck Rogers stuff would come in handy one day."

"Shut up," said Connie affectionately, tucking her maroon blouse into her pleated skirt. "So where the hell do we get actors to play Zontac and Korkhan at the eleventh hour?"

"Search me. What a minute. Saul's poker table. Manny used to do stand-up comedy. Terry once appeared off-Broadway in *R.U.R.*"

"What about their dialogue? Improvisation?"

"Cue cards. Like we do with those uppity radio actors who refuse to learn their lines."

"We'll need costumes."

"I'm thinking of an early *Tell Me a Ghost Story*," I said. " 'Revenge of the Gargoyles,' 'Curse of the Gargoyles,' 'Gargoyles of Sunnybrook Farm,' something like that."

" 'Night of the Gargoyles,' " said Connie. "Script by brother Howard. He hated how Sonny Glover directed it."

"But the masks were terrific. As for Ralston Purina, the *Corporal Rex* commercial is always done live. We'll simply drop it into our show at ten forty-five."

"Brilliant!"

An instant later I deactivated the alarm clock and tossed it into my valise. Fully clothed now, Connie and I slipped out of Studio Three and dashed to the miniscule office she commanded as *Bread Alone*'s producer. I placed a call to 59 West 82nd Street. Saul answered with a chipper, "Bathsheba's Cathouse, King David speaking."

"Hi, Saul. It's me. How's it going?"

"That Volavont is one stud-poker-playing sonofa-bitch."

"Question. Did Manny and Terry look at the teleplay?"

"Furtively, like foxes," said Saul. "They like the idea of saving two million Christians, but they noticed the *Weltanschauung* problem."

"I think we've solved it, a matter of getting the lobsters to realize they're trafficking in nihilism. We're adding a whole half-hour, including *roman-à-clef* characters based on Wulawand and Volavont. Listen, Saul, you gotta convince Manny and Terry to show up here in a few hours. They were born to play Zontac and Korkhan."

"I don't understand—will they be ad-libbing? Isn't that risky?"

"Cue cards. Tell 'em that, if they come through for Connie and me, you'll publish their next stories sight unseen."

"Bribery is against my principles."

"Hey, Saul, we've got a chance to stop nihilism from infecting the whole goddamn Milky Way! Tell 'em you'll publish their next goddamn stories!"

"If I know Manny and Terry, they'll join your troupe for the fun of it."

"I want you to equip 'em with a couple of toy rayguns from your collection. Conference room C. Eight o'clock. They should use the employees' entrance. Can you remember all that?"

"You can trust me, Kurt. Bye, now. I'm sitting on a full house."

As I cradled the handset, Connie opened her desk drawer and grabbed a metal ring from which a dozen keys dangled like jellyfish tentacles. I followed her down the stairs to the basement wardrobe department. The door yielded to a brass key. A nude male mannequin, gelded like a choirboy, mutely greeted us. For the next half-hour we alternately scoured the shelves (which held scads of masks, wigs, hats, helmets, and crowns fitted over disembodied faceless heads) and pawed through the racks (where scores of coats, capes, gowns, suits, and zippered costumes hung like gibbeted prisoners). Our efforts were rewarded with a pair of latex gargoyle masks—bulging eyes, flared nostrils, pointed ears, bulbous tongues—and matching slate-gray jumpsuits.

Costumes in hand, we scurried down the corridor to the employees' subterranean entrance. As it happened, the guard on duty was Claude Moffet, erstwhile performer on the defunct *Dick Tracy* radio serial. I told him that around 8:00 A.M. two eminent American writers bearing toy rayguns would appear, and he should admit them posthaste.

Returning to street level, Connie and I deposited the

134

gargoyle outfits in dressing room A, along with a note to the *Bread Alone* wardrobe mistress explaining that she should suit up Mr. Glass and Mr. Murgeon the instant they arrived. We sprinted to the storage closets, where we procured a hundred blank cue cards, plus a box of grease pencils. As we staggered away, hugging bundles of pasteboard, Connie and I agreed that we needn't write any new lines for the minor characters of Peter and the leper. As for Cotter Pin and Sylvester Simian, we should keep their brawny human *alter egos* in reserve, for they might prove vital in deterring unwanted visitors during the broadcast.

Arriving in conference room C, Connie and I got to work. For ninety minutes, we batted potential speeches and possible stage directions back and forth like shuttlecocks. (Per Hollis's contract, we remembered to include additional Sugar Corn Pops and Ovaltine commercials.) Taking turns in the role of stenographer, fighting sleep with every clause and comma, we methodically transcribed our best ideas, so that each cue card became a piece in a jigsaw puzzle that, assembled, might conceivably influence the course of galactic history.

The plot was simple. After the Demivirgin Mary delivers the final line of act one—"If forced to choose between a planet I know to be real and a paradise I must take on faith, I would surely cry, 'Give me the Earth!' "— two malign creatures rocket in from Voidovia. Zontac and Korkhan explain that they've embarked on a grand tour of the Milky Way, following an itinerary that includes vaporizing everyone who doesn't share their one hundred percent deity-free worldview. Drawing forth their rayguns, they threaten Jesus, his mother, his apostle, and the leper. But then Brock Barton comes to the Judeans' rescue, arguing that the Voidovians' professed atheism is nothing of the kind.

"You've not rejected God at all," says the captain of the *Triton*. "You've turned him into *yourselves*. How theistic of you."

"You've not dismantled the Almighty's throne," adds Ducky Malloy. "You've made it your favorite easy chair. How pious of you."

"If God is a bad idea, then *playing* God is an even worse idea," says Brock. "You invertebrates have embraced the very mythology you claim to despise."

"God is *not* a bad idea," Mary insists.

"It's a very *good* idea," Jesus avers.

"I think not," says Brock, having the last word.

Fade-out. Cut to title card, WHO CREATED GOD? Dissolve to NBC logo.

Under normal circumstances, Connie and I would now have borne the ninety-three new speeches to Studio Two and distributed them around the *Bread Alone* set. But our muscles and ligaments would hear none of it. Since Friday afternoon we'd been burning our candles at both ends; nothing remained of us but nubs of wax and smidgeons of wick. And so, after numbering the cue cards, we leaned them against the walls in a half-dozen upright stacks, crawled under the circular table, stretched out on the carpet, and promptly fell asleep, knowing that, sooner rather than later, a Judean theist, a *Triton* humanist, or a nihilistic gargoyle would rouse us from our slumbers.

5.
THAT BUCK ROGERS STUFF

Depressed by their poker losses, and to invertebrates no less, Manny Glass and Terry Murgeon had little desire to hang around Saul's apartment, and so they arrived in conference room C, rayguns at the ready, a half-hour ahead of schedule. As Connie and I crawled out from under the table, the two insomniac *Andromeda* writers presented us with catastrophic news. The picture tube of Saul's television set had burned out. Kaput. Defunct. Irredeemably on the fritz.

I grabbed the wall phone and, after quickly introducing Connie to "the pulp-meisters of Prospect Park," placed a frantic call to 59 West 82nd Street.

"You gotta borrow Gladys Everhart's TV!" I told Saul.

"She's at her sister's place in Yonkers, and I don't have a key to her apartment."

"Then go buy a new TV!"

"Agoraphobics don't go out and buy new TV's, Kurt, especially on Sunday morning. The stores aren't open."

"Call a repairman!"

"It's Sunday, Kurt! It's the *fershlugginer* Christian Sabbath!"

"Get the lobsters to steal one!"

"That would be a recipe for disaster," said Saul.

"Doing nothing about the Qualimosan death-ray is a recipe for disaster!"

"I'm on the case, Kurt," said Saul. *"Shalom."*

"So which is the better part?" asked Manny, rifling through a stack of cue cards. With his rapid-fire speech cadences and fondness for wisecracks, he was generally regarded as the Groucho Marx of pulp science fiction. "Zontac or Korkhan?"

"It depends on how you feel about facing two million *Bread Alone* viewers and declaring, 'Logical positivism today, logical positivism tomorrow, logical positivism forever!' " said Connie. "That's Zontac's best line."

"I think I'll play Korkhan," said Manny.

"Which gives you the speech that begins, 'Die, Judean scum!' " said Connie. " 'Go to your illusory maker, you deluded fools!' "

"Actually, I'm leaning toward Zontac," said Manny.

"Let's flip a coin." Terry pulled a nickel from his pocket and passed it to me. A pale man with a mellifluous voice, he was as suave and ethereal as Manny was ribald and earthy. "Heads, I'm stuck with Zontac. Tails, I'm forced to play Korkhan."

I flipped the coin. Terry would play Zontac.

"Listen, fellas," said Connie, "Kurt and I really appreciate how you stepped up to the plate at the last minute."

"I ask myself, if Kurt Jastrow and Connie Osborne ever got the opportunity to save a couple million Jews," said Manny, "like maybe the audience for *The Goldbergs*, would they rise to the occasion? I'm sure they would."

"Take the cue cards to Studio Two and distribute them around the set in chronological order," said Connie, gesturing toward the stacks of grease-pencil speeches. "Then find the switchboard cubby and tell Lulu she'll be receiving some irate calls this morning. In every case, she should say, 'Didn't you know? This is our once-a-year Saturnalia hoax.' "

"No, she should say, 'It's an April Fool's Day gag,' " Manny insisted. "When the caller says, 'But it's not April Fool's Day,' Lulu answers, 'That's part of the gag.' "

"I like that," said Terry.

Connie glowered and said, "Finally, go to dressing room A, where Hannah will zip you into your Voidovian suits. They're actually gargoyle costumes left over from an old *Tell Me a Ghost Story*."

"I saw that one," said Manny, opening the door for Terry. " 'Gargoyle Bar Mitzvah.' Very avant-garde."

No sooner did the *Andromeda* writers leave on their errands than conference room C began filling up with actors. True to his word, Ezra had brought along an ice chest jammed with a box of Sugar Corn Pops, a jar of Ovaltine, and a bottle of milk. Assuming a persona of authority, somewhere between a crossing guard and a softball coach, Connie removed her loafers and climbed atop the table.

"God willing, we are about to write a glorious chapter in the annals of anonymous benevolence," she told the assembled company.

"Last night I read the Book of Job and cobbled together a nifty little rant," said Gully.

"I'll try to shoehorn it in," Connie assured him.

"I'm all set to endorse Jesus's preferred Eucharist substances," said Hollis.

"You're also our announcer," said Connie. "The final image is a midshot of two chastened aliens, so you'll have no problem getting to the booth in time for the closing signature."

"Chastened aliens?" said Clement. "That isn't in my script."

"Mine neither," said Wilma.

"Same here," said Jimmy.

Connie proceeded to explain that, during the night, "The Madonna and the Starship" had transmuted into a fifty-five minute epic. The pivot from act one to act two would occur on Mary's line about preferring a real planet to a hypothetical paradise. When writing the second half of the show, Connie continued, she and Mr. Jastrow had focused on convincing the Qualimosans that their worldview was unworthy of the term "logical positivism," for it was as barbaric in its attack on conventional wisdom as Friedrich Nietzsche's had been erudite. The troupe would find the additional material—including speeches by invading aliens Zontac and Korkhan, plus new dialogue for Brock, Ducky, Jesus, and Mary—displayed on a convenient panorama of cue cards. Peter and the leper could, if they wished, contribute an occasional extemporaneous line. As for Cotter Pin and Sylvester, it would be best if the corresponding actors slipped away shortly after ten-thirty and started guarding the periphery of the set, for by then the broadcast would have surely drawn a mob of protestors.

"So we're gunning for their *Weltanschauung* after all!" exclaimed Ezra. "Marvelous!"

"And how are the producers of *Corporal Rex* taking all this?" asked Calder.

"Except for the commercial, the whole show's on 35mm celluloid," said Connie. "Film chains break down at the worst times—don't they, Joel?"

"I'm on the job," said the gorilla.

"And now, troupers, it's up and at 'em!" cried Connie. "Off with your clothes and into your costumes! I want to see everyone in Studio Two by nine-thirty on the dot!"

While our players transformed themselves into Judeans and Rocket Rangers, Connie and I hied ourselves to the

NBC commissary, where we consumed a couple of jelly doughnuts washed down with black coffee.

"About last night," she said, a line I'd vowed never to write if I ever became a real dramatist. "We both went a little crazy, huh? The tech rehearsal, the exhaustion, the kaleidoscopes. What I'm trying to say is that I'm not in the market for a steady boyfriend."

"I understand," I muttered, attempting to project simple disappointment but probably sounding despondent. "That prism takes a person to the strangest places."

"My analyst says that now's the time for me to concentrate on my career. Believe me, Kurt, if I *wanted* a relationship, you'd be at the top of the list—"

"Ahead of Sidney Blanchard?"

"Way ahead of Sidney, but for the next several years I want to throw myself into scriptwriting. Okay, sure, *Bread Alone* is doomed. Religious broadcasting? It's here to stay, and I want to help it grow. Thanks to 'The Madonna and the Starship,' I've started seeing unexpected possibilities in the form."

"Unexpected," I said, finishing my coffee. "Makes sense. Now let's go run those pesky Martians out of town."

"Will Mr. Silver figure out how to get them in front of a functional TV?" asked Connie.

"He's pulled bigger rabbits out of smaller hats."

Resuscitated, though hardly revitalized, I followed Connie as she dashed to the kinescope booth, the facility through which NBC preserved its most important broadcasts for posterity. The television monitor and the loaded 35mm camera faced each other like gunfighters in Dodge City, while the auxiliary shutter stood ready to resolve the disparity—thirty frames per second versus twenty-four—between the respective optical illusions on which television and motion pictures depended. The technician hadn't arrived yet, so Connie left him a note saying that this morning's *Bread Alone* must not be committed to celluloid. *It's certain to be our worst show ever,* she wrote, *and I want it to leave no trace.*

We exited the kinescope booth, sprinted to Studio Two, and waded into the hubbub: the lighting director fiddling with his kliegs and fresnels, the boom operator adjusting his omnidirectional mike, the cameramen rehearsing their dolly moves, the floor manager pacing nervously around, the assistant director pursuing an equally anxious path—and everyone casting puzzled glances at the costumed gargoyles, wondering why Ogden Lynx had imported two medieval statues into a drama set in ancient Palestine. All ninety-three cue cards fringed the dining-room set. The on-air floor monitor displayed the current NBC offering: a live puppet show out of Studio Three called *Locky the Loch Ness Monster*. Although the image was almost certainly a closed-circuit feed, uncoupled from the carrier wave, I resolved to kill this particular cathode-ray tube when "The Madonna and the Starship" began, just to make sure we eluded the death-ray.

Connie whistled sharply, commanding the crew's attention, then revealed that this morning's broadcast would be "a trifle unorthodox." No matter what the actors said—no matter what they did or what costumes they wore—"each of you professionals must stay at his post." Sooner rather than later, she insisted, the program's ostensible irreverence would be "explained to everyone's satisfaction."

The instant Connie finished her speech, an unwelcome visitor appeared, the eternally crusty Ogden, dressed in his usual loud checked jacket and polka-dot bowtie, cricketing his way across the studio floor like some immense insect out of a *Brock Barton* episode.

"Morning, Connie," he said. "I decided to drop by and help out."

"Know how you can help?" said Connie. "Go home."

"I promise not to kibitz unless you ask."

"What I'm asking is for you to leave."

"See here, Connie Osborne!" shouted Ogden. "I've directed forty-one consecutive *Bread Alone* installments! This is *my* show, too!"

Now the program's regular announcer, the lumpish and genial Fred Thigpen, ambled into view.

"Hi, Mr. Lynx, morning, Miss Osborne—sorry I'm late. Where's the script?"

"Guess what, Mr. Thigpen?" said Connie. "We won't be employing your services today. It's our once-a-year Saturnalia celebration."

"Saturnalia?" said Ogden.

"But this is Sunday," said Fred.

"Bingo," said Connie. "Go to church, Mr. Thigpen. Read the funnies. Mow your lawn. Report for work this time next week."

The bewildered announcer shrugged and sauntered away.

While Connie and Ogden resumed their argument, I climbed the stairs to the control room, where Leo the technical director and Harold the audio engineer practiced their cross-fades and twiddled their potentiometers. I grabbed the telephone and called Saul.

"Okay, problem solved," he said: a felicitous message— so why did he sound distressed? "I just finished escorting the lobsters—"

"Escorting them? You mean you left your apartment?"

"I took 'em all the way to Marty's Electronics Shop on Eighty-Fourth. We broke in, found a working Zenith, turned the dial to channel two, tuned in a puppet show called—"

"*Locky the Loch Ness Monster*!" I cried. "Brilliant, Saul! I'm damned impressed! You triumphed over your condition!"

"I didn't triumph over anything! I got to hear Wula-wand contact her orbiting navigator and make sure the death-ray was still on standby alert, but then I bailed out, leaving the lobsters with their Zenith." A mournful sigh escaped Saul's throat. "Want to know something, Kurt?

I crawled—that's right, I fucking *crawled* back home! Me, the editor of a respected literary magazine, inching his way down Amsterdam Avenue on hands and knees!" He released a groan compounded of equal parts humiliation and pique. "Lucky for me, a cop happened by and helped me up the stairs to my apartment. Right now I'm under my desk with Zelda and Zoey."

"What a heroic effort," I said, even as nausea gripped my innards. With Saul and the lobsters in different zones, we'd have no way of knowing whether, when Wulawand talked to Yaxquid for a second time that morning, she'd ordered the slaughter or canceled it.

"I even remembered to tell the Qualimosans to stick around for the second half-hour," said Saul. "Gotta go, Kurt. I'm about to *plotz.*"

Bit by bit, a scheme took shape in my brain. I bolted from the control room, told Connie the good news about Marty's Electronics Shop—she was still squabbling with Ogden—and fled the *Bread Alone* hurly-burly. Galvanized by my memories of the death-ray murdering the dressmaker's dummy, I proceeded to the wardrobe department, where I appropriated the male mannequin. I trundled the thing to Studio One. The Motorola in Uncle Wonder's attic was exactly as we'd left it on Friday afternoon, rabbit ears connected, studio-feed spade lug lying disconnected on the floor.

I set the mannequin directly in front of the picture tube, then rigged the AC cord with a piece of twine so I could cut the power if and when the death-ray emerged from the scanning-gun. Gingerly I switched on the Motorola, turned the dial to NBC, and tuned in *Locky the Loch Ness Monster*. By my lights, at least, I had just devised the perfect mechanism for determining whether, come 10:10 A.M. or thereabouts, two million TV viewers had been spared or roasted. Uncle Wonder a.k.a. Kurt Jastrow was a clever fellow indeed.

Returning to Studio Two, I glanced at the dormant red ON THE AIR light hanging above the portal, with its implicit addendum, ABANDON HOPE ALL YE WHO INTER-RUPT. In five minutes the floor manager would ignite the sign. Under normal circumstances this directive reliably deterred unwanted intruders, but it would surely prove impotent against God's partisans—and yet I felt vaguely confident that our robot and our gorilla could keep them at bay through the end of act one and possibly beyond.

Connie and Ogden had relocated their altercation to the control room. I approached the on-air floor monitor, which currently displayed the final shot of *Locky the Loch Ness Monster* (a plesiosaur puppet sitting in a bathtub, playing volleyball with a rubber duck), and reached for the on-off knob. The *Locky* end title dissolved into a commercial for a doll called Mop Top. I extinguished the picture tube (thereby perhaps preventing the X-13 from wreaking havoc in the studio), then climbed the stairs to the director's domain. Peering through the glass, I surveyed the scene below.

Smartly outfitted in his Brock Barton dress blues, complete with an embroidered gold comet on the breast, Hollis strode to the announcer's booth. Clothed in a hooded robe, Wilma sat at the dining table, fidgeting under the gaze of camera three, the boom mike suspended above her head like low-hanging fruit. Squinting at the cue cards, the other players milled about the periphery of the set. Calder's robot costume was a triumph of science-fictional design, a kind of Italian futurist salt-shaker with limbs and eyes. Joel's gorilla suit appeared extraordinarily authoritative. He was obviously the sort of primate who, when lecturing on Darwinian evolution, held his audience spellbound.

"You're planning something subversive, Connie!" seethed Ogden. "I can *tell!*"

"Put a sock in it, Ogden!" said Connie. "I'm trying to direct a goddamn TV show!"

The console's camera-one monitor displayed the standard NOT BY BREAD ALONE title card, beautifully lettered in Old English script, as did the preview monitor, while the camera-two monitor offered a sign reading, THE MADONNA AND THE STARSHIP. Harold the audio engineer stood poised over the turntable, ready to drop the needle on the show's familiar theme, Schubert's "Ave Maria." Connie put on her headset and sat down before the console. Leo the technical director darkened the on-air monitor, then punched in camera one. I checked my wristwatch. 9:59 A.M. God help us all.

"Music," said Connie as Studio Two went on the air.

"Ave Maria" flooded the control room and a myriad North American living rooms.

"Up on camera one," said Connie.

Leo performed a quick fade-in, so that the words NOT BY BREAD ALONE filled the on-air monitor and two million corresponding television sets.

"Cue the host," said Connie.

The floor manager pointed toward the announcer's booth.

"NBC proudly presents stories alerting viewers to the ways that people of faith," intoned Hollis, "whether living in ancient Judea or modern America, have impoverished their intellects with supernatural explanations of reality, for a mind cannot thrive on self-delusion any more than a body can live by bread alone."

"What the hey?" said Ogden.

"Dissolve to two," said Connie.

Leo cross-faded from the title card to camera two's image, the sign heralding THE MADONNA AND THE STARSHIP.

"Stay tuned for this morning's special one-hour tele-play, 'The Madonna and the Starship'!" enthused Hollis.

"One hour?" rasped Ogden. "What about *Corporal Rex*?"

"Music out," said Connie. "Up on three."

Leo executed a fade-out, punched in camera three, and brightened the on-air monitor, delivering a midshot of Wilma to the airwaves.

"Cue Mary."

The floor manager pointed at Wilma, who launched into her opening lament.

"On Friday they murdered my son, the rabbi. My first-born boy. Nailed to a tree like a jackal pelt, just because he called for the immediate and violent overthrow of the Roman Empire."

"Camera two, give me a longshot," said Connie.

"So here I am in Lazarus's dining room, sitting shivah," said Mary. "That's seven days of mourning for you *goyim* out there. Nobody showed up on the Sabbath, but I'm optimistic about today."

"Cut to two," said Connie.

The apostle Peter strode onto the set. Placing a comforting hand on Mary's shoulder, he revealed that, by saturating Jesus's vinegar sponge with an opiate, he'd persuaded the Roman centurions that the convicted seditionist had died on the cross.

"This is outrageous!" cried Ogden.

"Shut up!" said Connie.

"Any minute now, the drug will wear off," said Peter to Mary. "Jesus should have no trouble tearing free of his shroud and rolling back the stone."

"Camera three, tight on the tomb," said Connie.

"Naturally I'm delighted that my boy is about to return," said Mary. "But I fear your scheme will spark rumors of a resurrection."

"Stop the show!" yelled Ogden.

"Cut to three," said Connie.

As Jesus emerged from Arimathea's crypt, the control-room telephone rang. I grabbed the receiver, said "Hello," and listened politely as Walter Spalding told me to put Ogden on the line.

"Miss Osborne's directing this morning," I replied.

"Then put *her* on the line!" shouted NBC's normally phlegmatic head of programming.

"Didn't you hear me? She's *directing.*"

"Who's this?"

"Kurt Jastrow."

"Hey, Kurt, what the hell is going on over there?" asked Walter. "My Aunt Edna tuned in *Bread Alone* this morning. She was horrified, so she phoned me at the studio, and now *I'm* horrified."

"It's complicated," I said. "Heed my warning, Walter. You and Aunt Edna should switch to *Lamp Unto My Feet*, or you might get hit with an alien death-ray. Bye now."

"Jastrow!"

I slammed down the handset, then grabbed a pair of scissors and severed the phone line as neatly as a mayor cutting the ribbon at a construction site. There would be no more annoyance calls this morning.

I faced the console and contemplated the on-air monitor. Jesus shuffled into Lazarus's dining room, his shroud hanging limply from his shoulders, his wrists displaying nail wounds, then described his ordeal of waking up alive in a tomb. "The unendurable oppression of the lungs"—Connie and I had appropriated a passage from Poe's story about a premature burial—"the stifling fumes of the damp earth, the clinging to the death garments, the rigid embrace of the narrow house, the unseen but palpable presence of the conqueror worm."

After Jesus explained how he'd extricated himself from his shroud and dispensed with the stone, Mary casually remarked, per the White Horse Tavern rewrite of the rewrite, "As a little boy, you were quite a handful, especially compared to your two brothers."

"Well *naturally* I was a handful," noted Jesus. "I'm God, you know. Or is that my madness talking?"

Ogden dropped to his knees and began to pray.

"I wonder who worked harder, you raising me from a baby, or my Heavenly Father raising me from the dead?" said Jesus to his mother—an astute ad lib by Ezra.

Suddenly Brock Barton and three other Rocket Rangers burst onto the set. Availing himself of the fruit bowl, Ducky Malloy jammed a half-dozen plastic grapes in his mouth, then spat them on the floor like watermelon seeds. Cotter Pin grabbed three figs and started juggling them. Sylvester Simian sniffed Peter's neck and midriff.

"Greetings, pathetic Judeans!" Brock declared. "The

star sailors and I have traveled an entire light year to prevent yet another religion from contaminating the Milky Way!"

"I've been from one end of this galaxy to the other," added Cotter Pin in his static-laden *basso profundo* voice, "and I can tell you that, once a new church gets up to speed, the news is normally bad. On Alpha Centauri-3 they're burning female herbalists even as we speak. On Gliese Omicron-4 it's now open season on heretics."

"I wish all the races in the Milky Way would become logical positivists," said the gorilla.

"Or at least illogical positivists," said Ducky.

"But surely reason and science have a dark side, too," said Mary, a line on which Connie had insisted.

"Not dark enough to keep me up at night," said Brock, a riposte that I'd demanded.

"Harold, kill the boom mike!" ordered Ogden, regaining his feet. "Leo, stand by to bring up the film chain! We're switching to Hopalong Cassidy!"

"Kurt, dear, it's time you escorted Mr. Lynx out of here," said Connie.

I didn't have to drag Ogden away, because he left of his own accord, headed for NBC's trove of westerns. As I followed him down the control-room stairs, Joel deftly assessed the situation and sidled out of camera range. Together the gorilla and I chased Ogden as he ran through the studio door, then along the corridor toward the film-chain closet.

Arriving in the claustrophobic space, Ogden scanned the racks of 35mm prints, looking for a Hopalong Cassidy vehicle. Joel crashed into the closet, removed his ape mask, and wrenched the camera free of the floor, tucking it under his arm like a Frenchman transporting a baguette. Under no circumstances would *Corporal Rex* preempt our planned preemption of it.

"How *dare* you!" cried Ogden.

"Go home, Mr. Lynx, or I'll put your head in a wrestling lock of my own invention," said Joel. "I call it Madame Guillotine."

"NBC will be sending you a repair bill!" wailed Ogden.

"Not before Beth Israel sends you an emergency room bill!" screamed Joel.

Having lost the skirmish, Ogden threw up his hands and stalked off. An instant later the film-chain operator, a pot-bellied technician whose name I could never remember, appeared bearing two large hexagonal canisters labeled *Wonder Dog Episode 23.*

"No *Corporal Rex* today, Lou," said Joel, pointing to the uprooted camera. Louis, that was his name. "The vidicon just went haywire."

"Haywire?" said Louis. "What do you mean?"

"Not to worry," I said. "My *Bread Alone* teleplay runs till eleven o'clock in Studio Two."

"Don't you usually write that Buck Rogers stuff?" Louis asked me.

"I'm branching out."

"Ralston Purina will bust a gusset."

"Everything's under control," I said. "At ten forty-five we'll dissolve to the usual live commercial."

" 'Fraid I gotta run," said Joel, restoring his gorilla mask. "Big speech coming up. Tell me, Lou, what's your opinion of Charles Darwin?"

"He the guy plays second banana on *Tales of the Pony Express*? Not much of an actor."

Joel turned to me and said, "Hey, Kurt, how do you think it's going?"

"Better than I expected." I glanced at my watch. 10:08 A.M. "Uncle Wonder's Motorola is receiving the broadcast. Two or three minutes from now, we'll know if the Martians bought our act."

"Don't get yourself incinerated," said Joel.

"I tied a string to the AC cord."

"What the hell are you two talking about?" asked Louis.

"Be careful, Kurt," said Joel. "Good TV writers are hard to find."

The sagacious ape pirouetted and hurried away, bearing the stolen camera.

Consider this thought experiment. A letter arrives in your mailbox—a message from your doctor that will reveal whether the lump in your armpit is malignant or benign. Imagine the trepidation with which you tear open the envelope. Now double that dread, and you'll appreciate my state of mind as I entered Studio One.

Heart pounding, palms sweating, I marched onto the attic set. The Motorola remained illuminated, calling down "The Madonna and the Starship" from the heavens. The male mannequin was still standing, seemingly absorbed in the broadcast. I took hold of the twine—one yank, and the scanning-gun would die—then gritted my teeth and consulted my watch. 10:10 A.M. Zero hour.

On the tube, Jesus solemnly shared bowls of cereal with the star sailors and the other Judeans. "Eat these measures of Sugar Corn Pops," he said, "for they are my body."

"You know, Jesus, the great thing about Sugar Corn Pops is that it's got the sweetenin' already on it," said Brock.

"Even tin men like the taste," said Cotter Pin.

"Most impressive," Jesus replied, methodically distributing eight mugs of warm, chocolate-flavored beverage. "Drink this Ovaltine, for it is my blood."

"My next-door neighbor's kid, little Sally Warren, was having a hard time in fifth grade," said Brock. "But then her mom started her on Ovaltine each morning, and Sally's grades rocketed through the roof. She also became a dodge-ball champion."

"I've heard that four out of five elementary school teachers recommend Ovaltine," said Jesus.

I checked my watch. 10:12 A.M. Success! Triumph! Deliverance! Hooray for Our Lady of Pompeii! Monitoring the show in Marty's Electronics Shop, Wulawand had contacted her spaceship and canceled the slaughter!

Well, maybe.

I couldn't help imagining scenarios that might prompt the automatic 10:20 A.M. triggering. Perhaps the aliens' Zenith had gone on the fritz, just like Saul's Admiral, and they'd been unable to see the broadcast. Maybe Wulawand's transceiver had conked out before she could deliver the cancelation order to Yaxquid. Conceivably Yaxquid, observing the show from the orbiting vessel, was finding it insufficiently satiric and, in defiance of Wulawand's command, had decided to let the death-ray fire of its own accord.

Each subsequent minute of "The Madonna and the Starship" seemed to consume an hour. Reeling with anxiety, I watched the blind and crippled leper enter Lazarus's house and beg Jesus for a miracle cure. At 10:14 A.M. the Galilean rabbi attempted to heal the unfortunate man's scabrous skin, dysfunctional eyes, and paralyzed leg. By 10:16 A.M. it was clear that the rehabilitation attempt had failed, and so the leper climbed gingerly onto the breakaway dining table and cursed the Almighty with quotations from the Book of Job, including "When a sudden deadly scourge descends, God laughs at the plight of the innocent!" and "From the towns come the groans of wounded men crying for help, yet God remains deaf to their appeal!" At 10:19 A.M. the leper descended from the table, whereupon Sylvester Simian began lecturing the Judeans, asserting that the geological, paleontological, anatomical, and embryological evidence for materialist evolution was overwhelming. An irritated Jesus and an equally unhappy Peter responded by smashing Lazarus's table and chairs to pieces and converting the debris into cudgels.

I glanced at my watch. Twenty-two minutes after ten! We were out of the woods! We'd saved two million lives!

As the brawl progressed, I switched off the Motorola, kissed the mannequin's cheek, and gleefully exited the attic set. I dashed down the corridor to Studio Two, then scrambled up the stairs to Connie's realm. At some point Walter Spalding had arrived in the control room, and now he stood propped against an oscilloscope, gagged with a bandana, bound hand-and-foot with gaffer tape. (Presumably Joel had tied him up, then vaulted onto the set just in time to deliver his speech.) Absorbed in directing the brawl, Connie took no note of my arrival. Instead she cut from a longshot of Lazarus's wrecked dining room—broken furniture, shattered fruit bowl, fractured amphorae, toppled potted palm, shards of communion crockery—to a midshot of Jesus banging on Cotter Pin's aluminum chest with a table leg.

"Uncle Wonder's Motorola has been receiving NBC all morning!" I cried. "Nothing happened! The scanning-gun never fired!"

Although my message must have been meaningless to them, Leo the technical director and Harold the audio engineer burst into applause. Connie rose from the console, tore off her headset, and kissed me on the lips.

"Evidently the lobsters loved it all!" I gushed. "The fake resurrection, the Sugar Pops Eucharist, the leper's rant, the atheist gorilla—everything!"

"Walter just told me I'm out of a job, and right now I don't care." Connie restored her headset and sat down again. "Camera three, let's see Mary in close-up. Ready? Cut to three."

"I shall abandon neither the God of my Fathers nor the Supreme Being of my Mothers!" proclaimed Our Lady, shouting above the mêlée. Gradually the commotion abated. The Judeans and the Rocket Rangers accorded Mary their full attention. "And yet I am pleased that Brock Barton and his friends came into my life," she continued. "If forced to choose between a planet I know to be real and a paradise I must take on faith, I would surely cry, 'Give me the Earth!' "

Connie cut back to a longshot. Waving their rayguns around, two creatures from Planet Voidovia dashed into Lazarus's dining room. The second act had begun.

Initially things went amazingly well. Manny and Terry made excellent nihilists, alternately reading cynical dialogue and improvising sardonic lines.

"Should I spare your life, O Jesus Christ?" said Terry, speaking off-the-cuff as he pointed his raygun at Ezra. "I think not. We rationalists have proved that compassion is a swindle."

"Of all the human sentiments, none is more pathetic than pity, O Mary Mother of the Alleged God," ad-libbed Manny, threatening the Madonna with his weapon. "Ask Friedrich Nietzsche."

"I wish he'd leave Nietzsche out of it," said Connie.

Suddenly Ogden Lynx came charging through the door and headed toward Lazarus's dining room. Behind him surged three men and three women, dressed in their Sunday best and wielding placards bearing hostile sentiments. BROCK BARTON IS JUDAS ISCARIOT ... NBC EQUALS NATIONAL BLASPHEMY CORPORATION ... METHODISTS AGAINST MOCKERY ... BANISH ATHEISTS FROM THE AIRWAVES ... GIVE US THE REAL "BREAD" ... NO REDS IN OUR LIVING ROOMS. After our film-chain dustup, Ogden had apparently run to the nearest church, crashed the ten o'clock service, and recruited a band of congregants to his cause.

"Get those goddamn Methodists out of here!" Connie instructed me.

Already Calder and Joel were on the move. As I left the control room and charged down the stairs, our robot and our gorilla armed themselves with orphaned legs from Lazarus's table and formed a fleshy redoubt against the invasion.

"Shame on all of you!" shouted a male protestor, an imprecation surely heard by the viewers at home, assuming they'd not been barbecued.

"End this travesty now!" yelled a female Methodist.

"Cease and desist!" Ogden demanded.

Now another contingent entered the studio: a poodle, an Irish setter, a cocker spaniel, a boxer, and a collie—followed by a lantern-jawed dog handler wearing TV makeup and an NYPD uniform. He pushed a motorcycle sidecar holding a sack of Purina kibble, two unlabeled bags, and a stack of aluminum bowls.

"I'm Hank Griswold," the dog handler told me, then gestured toward the protestors. "Who the hell are they?" He led his four-legged actors toward the back of the studio, evidently the locus of the live Ralston Purina commercial around which every *Corporal Rex* episode revolved. "In five minutes the gang and I are on the air." Without being told, the dogs lined up before the gold curtain. "I'm fine with your *Brock Barton* rehearsal, but that pro-McCarthy demonstration has got to go."

"I imagine your canine friends share that opinion," I said, raising an eyebrow.

"I see what you're getting at." Hank extended an index finger, touching each dog on its nose, then pointed to the demonstrators. "Sadie, Liam, Charlie, Spike, Duchess—repel prowlers!"

With an exuberant howl, Sadie the poodle lunged at Ogden, even as Liam the setter, Charlie the spaniel, Spike

162

the boxer, and Duchess the collie selected one protester apiece and menaced them with snarls and snapping jaws. Cotter Pin and Sylvester Simian singled out the remaining intruders, the robot intimidating his Methodist by shifting his eyeballs into flashing-pinwheel mode, the gorilla rattling his nemesis with the most bloodcurdling roar ever to issue from a vegetarian vertebrate.

Sputtering, moaning, and tripping over cables, Ogden and his entourage ran pell-mell out of the studio. The dogs issued a final chorus of barks, then turned and pranced back to their marks.

I remained on the floor, my mind still awhirl from our apparent victory over the death-ray. The rest of "The Madonna and the Starship" rushed by in a delirious swish-pan blur. I retain no connected memories of that frenzied interval, only discrete vignettes: the live commercial, the script of which required the dogs to turn up their noses at "the other two leading brands," then eagerly devour their Purina kibble, "the chow that makes Corporal Rex the Wonder Dog he is," as Hank put it (though I later learned that the other two leading brands were chunks of gravel) ... Brock arguing, per the script for act two, that if God was a bad idea, then *playing* God was an even worse idea ... Zontac and Korkhan in midshot, the former saying, "O Brock Barton, we now see that our worldview partakes of a toxic nihilism," the latter pleading, "O Ducky Malloy, help us to outgrow our puerile preoccupation with the void"... Jesus casually mentioning to Peter that he intended to start feeding Purina to his sheepdog ... Hollis rushing into the announcer's booth and declaring, "Tune in next Sunday for another iconoclastic installment of *Not By Bread Alone*! Our forthcoming presentation is an original teleplay by Robert Ingersoll, 'If God Created the Universe, Then Who Created God?' "

At long last—could it be? was it possible?—the whole mad circus was over, and there stood Connie, leaning against the floor monitor, dazed and haggard, a tiara of sweat speckling her brow, and over there slouched our tired but magnificent cast, still in their costumes—Madonna, robot, leper, Messiah, apostle, ape, spaceship captain, sidekick, Voidovians—fidgeting amid the ruins of Lazarus's dining room, and farther still sat Walter Spalding, recently sprung from his gaffer-tape prison, wearing the trinocular goggles and staring into the iridescent depths of a Zorningorg Prize kaleidoscope. Connie switched on the floor monitor. NBC's normal 11:00 A.M. live broadcast of *Meet the Press* came streaming out of Studio One. So far, at least, the network had survived our heterodox teleplay. Phosphor dots danced across the picture tube, limning the Secretary of State, John Foster Dulles. God was in his heaven. Eisenhower was in his White House. Life went on.

"According to the Motorola in Studio One," Connie told the cast and crew in a hoarse voice, "there's every reason to believe we've prevented a pancontinental atrocity."

"We may have even purged nihilism from the Milky Way," I added.

"Connie, you're a genius," said Wilma.

"Kurt, we love you," declared Joel.

"Mission accomplished," proclaimed Gully.

"With the sweetenin' already on it," added Hollis.

"See you in the unemployment line," said Ezra.

"Now take your scripts home and burn 'em!" cried Connie. "As far as we're concerned, this broadcast never happened!"

Although exhausted, famished, and much in need of a nap followed by a shower, Manny and Terry nevertheless heroically ministered to Connie and myself—for we were obviously even wearier, hungrier, and grimier. After descending to the sub-basement and incinerating the cue cards in the NBC furnace, my *Andromeda* colleagues ferried us by Yellow Cab east across the river to Brooklyn, the corner of Flatbush Avenue and Fenimore Street. Wheezing and groaning, Connie and I followed the pulp-meisters up five flights of stairs to Terry's apartment.

I staggered into the kitchen, grabbed the telephone, and called Saul Silver.

"Planet Mongo, Ming the Merciless speaking," he answered.

"Glad you're feeling better, Saul. Hey, I think we did it. Did we do it?"

"The lobsters returned a half-hour ago. I asked Wulawand, 'So, my dear, when you contacted your orbiting friend, what did you tell him: thumbs up or thumbs down?' And Wulawand said, 'O Saul Silver, I am not yet ready to discuss this matter with you.' So I said, 'Why not?' And she said, 'The program was not at all what Volavont and I expected.'"

I didn't like the sound of that, not one bit, but then I described my mannequin-cum-Motorola experiment. Relating the outcome made me feel better, and Saul proceeded to corroborate my optimism. "Such a brilliant test you devised, Uncle Wonder," he told me. "Evidently no Christians were cremated this morning."

"Put Wulawand on the line."

Twenty seconds elapsed. Thirty seconds. Saul retrieved the handset and said, "She's not ready to talk to *you* either."

"Listen, we ended up at Terry's place. We need sleep and a square meal. Expect us around eight o'clock tonight, okay?"

"Sure, Kurt. And now it's back to the slush pile for me and the lobsters. Wulawand has a real knack for separating the gold from the dross."

I wandered into the living room and reported what I'd just learned to Connie and the pulp-meisters.

"The show wasn't what the lobsters expected?" said Connie. "What could that mean?"

"I don't want to think about it," I said.

"Me, I'm feeling terrific," said Manny. "If North America were on fire, we'd have heard by now."

After gathering together every quilt, blanket, spread, and comforter in the apartment, Terry assembled a quartet of sleeping bags on his living-room floor. At noon the conversation phase of our pajama party ended, and the four of us collapsed. My dreams took me to Studio One, where the *Brock Barton* troupe was rehearsing a script of mine that everyone found infuriating, largely because all the characters came from *Hedda Gabler*.

Six hours later I awoke. Connie and the pulp-meisters were already up and about, gorging themselves on a home-delivered deli order: bagels, lox, cheese blintzes, pastrami sandwiches, potato salad. A recent shower had left Connie looking pristine and dewy. She wore a Maid Marian outfit that Terry had thoughtfully stolen while returning his gargoyle costume to the wardrobe department. I took a shower, then eagerly joined the feast.

Terry reported that he'd telephoned a friend in the Bronx, who had in turn called his sister, a devotee of *Not By Bread Alone*. Although she'd found "The Madonna and the Starship" distressing, the broadcast had done her no physical harm.

"I'm ready to declare victory," said Manny.

As darkness cloaked the five boroughs, we descended to street level, hailed a cab, and returned to Manhattan. At my request the driver deposited us on the corner of Amsterdam and West 82nd Street. I proceeded to Saul's favorite bodega, a twenty-four-hour establishment that reputedly had an arrangement with the local cops concerning the Sunday blue laws. After borrowing a twenty from Connie, I bought two packages of brie and three bottles of Chianti. *In vino veritas,* I figured, applied no less to extraterrestrials than to Earthlings.

Once again Gladys admitted us to Saul's sanctum. His busted Admiral TV now functioned as a credenza holding a pile of *Andromeda* submissions. The great man and the lobsters were absorbed in their work, navigating the slush, but they all proved amenable to attending an impromptu wine-and-cheese party. The festivities began with Saul proposing a toast.

"L'Chaim!" he declared. "To life!"

"L'Chaim!" everyone echoed, pulp-meisters and TV writers and invertebrates alike, clicking their glasses together.

The first two bottles of *vino* went down quickly, and then came the *veritas,* while Ira the fox terrier worked the room, begging for brie.

"We spent the first two hours following the broadcast in a state of utter perplexity," Wulawand informed Connie and myself. "At the last minute, they changed the name of the program from *Not By Bread Alone* to *Lamp Unto My Feet*—but that is not why we became confused. You had told us to expect a satiric show, and it was nothing of the kind."

"No, you saw *Not By Bread Alone,*" I said. "Connie

and I watched the broadcast in Terry's apartment. We thought 'The Madonna and the Starship' was deliciously satiric."

"No, we saw *Lamp Unto My Feet*," Wulawand insisted. "Today's presentation was a one-hour drama called 'Brother to the Earth,' very treacly and pious, all about a man named Saint Francis of Assisi."

"I don't understand," I said, turning to Saul. "You told me you'd tuned in a puppet show on channel four, *Locky the Loch Ness Monster*."

"Which always comes on right before *Not By Bread Alone*," added Connie.

"Channel four?" said Saul, uncorking the third bottle of Chianti. "No, Kurt, I told you channel *two*, the NBC affiliate."

"Channel two is the *CBS* affiliate," noted Manny.

"Really?" said Saul. "I thought NBC was two. Do I look like an expert? Mostly I watch professional wrestling on ABC."

"God damn it," I said.

"Okay, so I screwed up," said Saul. "You might remember I was having a bad morning. But I never told you the puppet show was about any Loch Ness Monster."

"The program in question was called *Zooabaloo*," said Volavont.

"Which always precedes *Lamp Unto My Feet*," said Connie, wincing.

"Right before the broadcast in question, we suspended

the impervious veil three feet in front of the Zenith,"
said Wulawand. "At ten minutes after ten, having
decided that 'Brother to the Earth' was as malevolently
metaphysical as a drama could be, I contacted Yaxquid
and told him Mr. Jastrow and Miss Osborne had
deceived us, so he should piggyback the death-ray onto
the carrier wave as planned. Our navigator said, 'I shall
pull the trigger in thirty seconds.'"

"But Yaxquid failed to carry out the command," said
Volavont. "Ten-eleven came and went. Peering around
the veil, we kept watching 'Brother to the Earth.' Ten-
twelve. Ten-thirteen. Ten-fourteen. And still we watched.
No death-ray emerged from the Zenith, which forced us
to infer that the hive of irrationalist vermin had not
been exterminated."

"Naturally I tried reaching Yaxquid, but he would
not answer," said Wulawand, fingering his Prometheus
pendant. "Again I called the spaceship. Our navigator
ignored us. By now it was ten twenty-five. Evidently Yaxquid had overridden the automatic firing of the X-13."

The Earthlings in the room exchanged freighted
glances. We were in the pulp zone—something amazing,
astounding, and fantastic had occurred. Only one
hypothetical chain of events could account for what the
lobsters were telling us. Obviously the orbiting navigator,
monitoring "The Madonna and the Starship" on channel
four, had determined that it was irreverent to a fare-thee-
well. When Wulawand and Volavont contacted him at

10:10 A,M. and ordered him to annihilate the show's viewers, he'd concluded that his fellow Qualimosans had lost their minds, or at least their senses of humor. And thus it was that, acting on his own initiative, Yaxquid disabled the death-ray.

"Remember the conversation we had about cultural crosstalk?" I asked the lobsters. "That show you saw, 'Brother to the Earth,' was intended to be sacrilegious."

"A jamboree of blasphemy," said Connie. "A circus of irreverence."

"Horse manure," said Wulawand.

"Bull feathers," said Volavont.

"So NBC is channel four and CBS is channel two," said Saul, replenishing everyone's wine glass. "I'll never make *that* mistake again."

"When you get back to Qualimosa," said Manny to the lobsters, "I guess you'll be tracking down Yaxquid and prosecuting him for insubordination."

"We are not returning to Qualimosa," said Volavont, sipping Chianti. "We are staying right here on your little blue planet."

"I don't understand," I said.

"O Kurt Jastrow, for reasons we cannot fathom, 'Brother to the Earth' impinged upon our affective nervous systems," said Wulawand. "Did you know that Saint Francis hugged lepers and gave away all his possessions to the poor? By the time the drama was over, we felt glad that Yaxquid had disobeyed us."

"Glad?" I said.

" 'The heart has reasons that reason knows not of,' " Connie quoted. "Pascal."

"O Connie Osborne, let me tell you about the time Saint Francis entered a deep wood, seeking an audience with a wolf who'd been attacking the residents of Gubbio." Wulawand took a substantial swallow of wine. " 'Your actions are those of a criminal, and in that regard you deserve to be hanged,' Saint Francis told the beast. 'However, I know you are driven by hunger, not spite. If the townspeople give you food every day, will you stop preying upon them?' The wolf lifted his right paw and laid it on Francis's open palm, thus making a pact with the saint and by extension the citizens of Gubbio. Week after week, month after month, the bargain held, and in time the townspeople canceled their plans to hunt down the wolf and slay him."

Volavont said, "Evidently Francis was influenced by the Galilean sage we learned about on Friday, back when *Lamp Unto My Feet* was called *Not By Bread Alone* and 'Brother to the Earth' was called 'Sitting Shivah for Jesus.' "

"And CBS was called NBC," said Manny.

"In our opinion," said Wulawand, "someone should expand the *Lamp Unto My Feet* cult into a worldwide organization dedicated to spreading the Galilean's selfless philosophy."

"It's been tried," said Terry, "but it didn't work out very well."

"And yet the spirit of Saint Francis endures," said Wulawand. "While Mr. Silver took his afternoon nap, Volavont and I put on our sandwich boards, rode the D train to Rockefeller Center, and consulted the computer in our shuttle. We soon acquired much data about the Saint Francis of Assisi House in the Bowery."

"Enough to decide we wish to spend the rest of our lives working for that institution," said Volavont.

"The rest of your lives?" I said.

"Quite so," said Wulawand.

"We intend to become Assisians," said Volavont. "Logical positivist Assisians."

"Amazing," said Manny.

"Astounding," said Terry.

"Donna Dain will be delighted," said Connie. "I guess you Qualimosans know about ethics after all."

"What is ethics?" said Wulawand.

"Never mind," said Connie.

"The manuscripts beckon," said Saul. "My slush runneth over. Let's get back to work."

Although we didn't know it at the time, the single smartest thing Connie and I did on the morning of the big broadcast was to call off the kinescoping. When ardent journalists and enraged viewers—the latter led by a Newark Baptist minister called Jerome Snavely—demanded to see the celluloid version of the notorious

Bread Alone episode, the NBC brass could reply, in all honesty, that no such record existed. One executive even summoned the *chutzpah* to declare that Reverend Snavely and his followers had "woefully misinterpreted" the presentation and were "filtering it through faulty memories and stunted imaginations."

Of course, the press and Snavely's flock insisted on seeing the mimeographed text of "The Madonna and the Starship." In every instance the network responded with a copy of Connie's original "Sitting Shivah for Jesus" script. Undaunted, Snavely spearheaded a letter-writing campaign. For three weeks angry epistles flooded the studio, but again the network refused to acknowledge that anything untoward had occurred, a policy that solidified into a doctrine after Floyd Cox's secretary noticed that over a third of the written protests focused less on the content of the broadcast than on its preemption of *Corporal Rex*.

As for Walter Spalding, the only network executive in the building when our psychotic Jesus took to the airwaves, he assumed the most radical stance of all. On the Sunday in question, he averred, a mysterious mass hallucination had afflicted thousands of Christians, and viewers who remembered the show as anything but reverent must be counted as victims of that syndrome. Walter's belligerence was easily explained. After gazing repeatedly into the alien prism and hearing my account of the Qualimosans, he'd become convinced that our rewrite had indeed saved two million lives.

The relevant sponsors were actually pleased with the fallout from "The Madonna and the Starship." As it happened, sales of Sugar Corn Pops and Ovaltine rose significantly after the broadcast. Connie and I speculated that the stodgier sort of *Bread Alone* devotee had never consumed these products in the first place, whereas the show's more open-minded viewers had found a bracing ecumenism in the replacement of the two traditional Eucharist species with a breakfast cereal and a malt beverage, and so they added these commodities to their shopping lists. Ralston Purina fared even better. Within hours of Jesus's declaration that he intended to feed their kibble to his sheepdog, the product began flying off supermarket shelves everywhere.

Thus did "The Madonna and the Starship" pass from scandal to anecdote, anecdote to legend, legend to oblivion. Defying the expectations of Connie and myself, *Not By Bread Alone*, *Brock Barton*, and *Uncle Wonder's Attic* remained on the air. When all three shows disappeared in the mid-sixties, the culprit was not sacrilege but low ratings. By this time, however, we were otherwise employed—Connie had become the chief administrator of the Saint Francis of Assisi House (Donna Dain having officially retired on her eightieth birthday), and I was working for NBC's latest experiment in SF television, *Star Trek*—and so we greeted the programs' passing with yearning rather than bitterness. Even as I pen this memoir, the Zorningorg

Prize sits on my desk, inspiring me to complete another Kirk-and-Spock adventure.

You may recall that, beyond my trophy, a second object attests to the strange week that elapsed between the Qualimosans' Monday afternoon appearance on Uncle Wonder's Motorola and our heroic troupe's Sunday morning effort to hoodwink them. I speak of the golden Prometheus statue in Rockefeller Center. As you now know, it's really a shapeshifted alien shuttle, though the lobsters once remarked that this startling fact cannot be verified through any sort of conventional chemical test or x-ray analysis.

In early April of 1955, three days after Saul accepted Connie's first attempt at a short story, "Do Not Go Gentle," for publication in *Andromeda*, she assented to my proposal of marriage. She still believed in God, and I still didn't, but we decided to give it a try anyway. (To this day she insists that, like Einstein, I believe in "the God of Spinoza," although *everybody* believes in the universe, as far as I know, so atheism versus Spinozism strikes me as a distinction without a difference.) When Connie's analyst objected to our impending union, she fired him. We were soon trading vows on the bridge of the *Triton*. Our ringbearer was Andy Tuckerman. Saul was cast as my best man, a role played collaboratively by Lenny and Eliot, his non-agoraphobic understudies. Hollis wore his Brock Barton dress blues, Calder his Cotter Pin outfit, Joel his gorilla suit, Ezra his Jesus robes, Manny and Terry their gargoyle costumes. Hank Griswold and his kennel also showed up—minus the Irish setter, who was recovering from knee surgery—as did Wulawand and Volavont, disguised as off-Broadway actors engaged in round-the-clock rehearsals for a musical adaptation of Kafka's *The Metamorphosis*.

It turned out I'd misjudged Andy Tuckerman. After Connie got to know the boy, she speculated that his sycophantic side might trace to a dysfunctional home life, and so she investigated. Her instincts proved correct. When Andy was six years old, his parents had died in an automobile accident—why had the network never told me this?—and his upbringing had devolved to an alcoholic aunt who regularly stole her nephew's TV earnings. Six months after our wedding, the adoption process finally ran its course, and Connie and I became Andy's mother and father.

One mystery remains. Did Yaxquid the navigator witness the entire broadcast? Or did he grab the spaceship's throttle the instant he decided that the *Bread Alone* audience couldn't possibly be thought pious? Connie and I like to believe that, after ignoring Wulawand's command and then disabling the death-ray, Yaxquid had stuck around for the second half of "The Madonna and the Starship," including the speeches by Brock and Ducky critiquing the Qualimosan worldview. Someday, after all, humankind will go to the stars. In the depths of space, Earthlings may encounter bug-eyed nihilists who murder fellow sentient life-forms in the name of some cynical ideology or other. But maybe, just maybe, thanks to Yaxquid's teachings, keyed to act two of our teleplay, all such monstrous *Weltanschauungs* will have vanished from our galaxy. Right now, of course, Connie and I have no way to determine the ontological status of meaninglessness in the Milky Way. We can only speculate, extrapolate, and submit fiction to Saul Silver.

For several years Wulawand and Volavont flourished in their calling as volunteers at the Saint Francis of Assisi House. They had no difficulty reconciling their Qualimosan rationality, now tempered by their "Brother to the Earth" encounter, with the benevolent ethos of the mission. What they couldn't abide was their own physiognomies. They hated looking so different from the other Saint Francis House personnel, and so they routinely submitted themselves to reckless procedures intended to transform their anatomies: untested drugs, Dr. Moreau-like surgeries, the shuttle's shapeshifting chamber—no intervention was too extreme.

Eventually our dear lobsters ended up in adjacent beds at Saint Vincent's Hospital, the institution where, a decade earlier, Dylan Thomas had drawn his last breath. Connie and I attended their final moments, seated on folding chairs between their ruined and recumbent forms. Wulawand and Volavont asked me to relate their favorite apocryphal episode from the life of Saint Francis. I squeezed Connie's hand and, with tears in my eyes and a catch in my voice, began telling them about the holy man negotiating with the marauding wolf.

" 'Let the citizens of Gubbio set out food for you,' " I said, quoting Saint Francis. " 'Accept their offerings, and they will have no cause to hunt you.' "

"And the bargain held," said Wulawand.

"Year after year," said Volavont.

"I don't want to leave!" declared Wulawand.

"L'Chaim!" cried Volavont.

"Eventually the wolf sickened with old age," I said. "The poor animal died in Saint Francis's arms."

Wulawand shrieked and closed her eyes, as did Volavont an instant later, and together they went raging into an ambiguous night.

"And for a long time afterward," I said, "the people of Gubbio were very sad."

ACKNOWLEDGEMENTS

The Madonna and the Starship traces to a series of conversations my wife and I enjoyed while she was researching the origins of American science fiction. At one point it occurred to me that, by steering a path between the nihilistic and the numinous—those dubious worldviews Western civilization so relentlessly recommends to its adherents—even the grottiest pulp SF performs a salutary cultural function. So, thank you, Kathryn Morrow, for igniting this project and reading the manuscript with such loving care. You are, now and forever, my best editor and favorite person.

Let me additionally offer my gratitude to those friends and colleagues who vetted early drafts of *The Madonna and the Starship*, noting anachronisms, technical gaffes, and stylistic infelicities. Whatever imperfections remain in this novella, they cannot be blamed on Joe Adamson, Peter Demski, Justin Fielding, Joseph Kaufman, Chris Morrow, Glenn Morrow, Bill Spangler, or Dave Stone, all of whom did their best to save me from myself.